DRAGON GUARD SCHOLAR

DRAGON GUARD SCHOLAR

Dragon Guard of the Northern Isles Book 2

ALICIA MONTGOMERY

CHAPTER 1

Ginny Russel drummed her fingers on her arm as she stood on the edge of a barren cliff overlooking the Norwegian Sea. As she watched the icy water churn and listened to the surf breaking along the rocks below, her chest tightened as if gripped in an invisible vise.

Her inner lioness paced, perhaps sensing the activation of her flight-or-fight response. But how could she tell it that the perceived threat was all in her head?

She willed her animal to stay calm. As long as she stayed up here, she could manage the tension building up inside.

Taking deep breaths, she closed her eyes and envisioned soothing places, like the stillness of Badain Jaran dunes of Mongolia or the Salar de Uyuni salt flats of Bolivia. Even thinking about the beautifully kept gardens of her childhood home in Colorado helped, despite the fact that she literally spent most of her adult life avoiding that place. When her body loosened up, she let out a sigh, and her lioness lay down in a relaxed position.

Glancing down at her wristwatch, she checked the time.

Still early. It was a short hike from the sleepy little village where she'd stayed the previous evening. Before that, she'd taken three flights, driven six hours, and took a ferry ride to get here. But in truth, she didn't mind the journey; that was the most exciting part of any trip for her. The exhilaration of travel never lessened, even now, in the tenth year of her nomadic life.

However, hopping from place to place and country to country for a decade did have its downsides, namely, she'd gone to almost every place she wanted. Traveling began to get boring, and for a while, she even thought it was time to settle down. In fact, she nearly did; two and a half years ago when she bought a one-way ticket back home. And that's when things changed.

Her lioness suddenly went on alert, sending the hairs on the back of her neck bristling. It knew, before she could hear or see it, that something approached. Something *big*.

There.

Her enhanced shifter sight spied the small dot in the distance, becoming bigger as it drew closer. Her animal's ears pricked forward, then flattened out as its tail lowered. This time, Ginny knew what it was first. Or rather, who.

Her lioness cowered.

Calm down.

It hissed at her, as if saying, *you try calming down when there's a humongous predator up there.*

But this wasn't a predator, at least, not any normal predator. No, this creature rushing toward them was special. One of the few dragon shifters in the world.

As it drew closer, the golden scales that covered the dragon's gigantic body gleamed. Its giant horned head swung around, searching for something, until its gaze landed straight on Ginny, then made a long arc to redirect its flight path. Leathery wings spread out, and it used the wind to glide, then slow down and descend toward the cliff.

She stepped back a few feet to give the dragon space as its clawed feet touched down on the rocky ground. The wind generated from its flapping wings nearly knocked her over, but she knew to dig in her heels to prevent herself from falling back.

The dragon began to shrink, its golden scaly body and giant horned head slowly disappearing until it was completely gone and only a dark-haired female stood in its place. "Hey, Ginny!" Sybil Lennox called as she slipped on the dress she had been carrying in her dragon's claws.

"What's up, Sybil?" she greeted back. "Long time no see."

Though Sybil Lennox was a few years younger than her, they'd known each other through their parents. Hank Lennox and Geraldine Russel had run in the same social and business circles, coming from two of the wealthiest and most influential shifter families in Colorado. Ginny recalled being invited to their castle for many birthday parties in her youth, and Sybil's older brothers Jason and Matthew had been in the same year as her brother Gabriel at Lucas Lennox High.

And now, apparently, she had married some king of a faraway land and ruled alongside him as queen. "Should I curtsy or bow, Your Majesty?"

Sybil approached, her silvery eyes rolling. "Ugh, no please. No formalities, at least not when we're alone. It's so nice to see you after all this time, Ginny! But I have to admit,

I was surprised when Christina told me who she was sending to help us. I didn't even know you were part of The Agency."

"I'm the one they call on when they need someone to sniff out secrets," she said with a wink.

During that fateful trip back two-and-a-half years ago, an anti-shifter organization had planted bombs in what she considered her home town—Blackstone. When she heard about the trouble, she volunteered to help sweep for bombs. It was a dangerous task, but during the entire time, there was an excitement and thrill she hadn't felt in years.

The town had been saved, and in the aftermath, she discovered the existence of The Shifter Protection Agency or simply, The Agency, run by Sybil's brother Jason Lennox and his wife, Christina. They had been so impressed with her investigation skills that they brought her in as one of their recruits, and after a solid year of training, started sending her out on missions.

Now when she traveled, she actually had a purpose. Though she'd done a variety of jobs for The Agency, undercover work seemed suited to her. Being pretty and petite helped, as few people suspected she had anything to hide, and putting on the dumb blonde act had gotten her out of more than a few scrapes. But she completed every mission assigned to her, and nothing satisfied her more than bringing justice to the helpless and oppressed of her kind.

When it came to jobs, she was relentless and never stopped until she finished her mission, then she moved onto the next. Her missions kept her grounded and in the present. Stopped her from dwelling on the past.

"Did Christina tell you why we need help?" Sybil asked.

"Yes, she briefed me on the situation," she replied,

grateful for the distraction. "You and your husband were attacked, and you suspect someone on the inside had something to do with it."

"Yes." Sybil's nostrils flared, and her eyes glowed briefly with the anger of her dragon. "We can give you more details when we get to the palace."

"Sure. When do we leave?"

Sybil chuckled. "Now."

"Now?" Ginny glanced around. "But how ... oh." *Oh fuck.* Her stomach flipped like a pancake. They were flying to the palace—via Dragon Airlines, apparently.

"Are you all right?" Sybil cocked her head to the side. "You don't mind, do you? The Northern Isles doesn't have any commercial flights or ferries, and if we flew you in with the jet, we'd have to explain why you were there. Aleksei thought it would be better if there was no record of your arrival since we still don't know who our mole is."

Ginny swallowed hard. "That makes sense. And no, it's no problem at all. I don't mind flying." No, flying wasn't the problem, after all. It was what was ahead, or rather, what they would be flying over.

The frigid, icy water stretching between them and their destination.

Her lioness backed away, snarling in displeasure, and Ginny couldn't even find the words to calm it down.

"Are you sure you're fine, Ginny? You look a little pale. I promise it's not a long flight. Just thirty minutes until we're over the main island."

"I'm sure," she said flatly, then turned on her heel to walk over to the rock where she had placed her backpack. "Ready when you are." Yet, the sweat beading on her forehead told her she'd never be ready. *As long as we fly high, I'll be fine.*

"Great. I'll grab onto you. I promise I won't let go."

"Thanks, I'm sure it'll be okay." It was *her* that was the problem, after all. With a deep breath, she secured her backpack to her body. Sure enough, when she turned around, Sybil was gone, and the dragon stood by the edge of the cliff. "Here goes nothing," she murmured under her breath.

Her lioness was calmer as they approached the dragon, perhaps sensing they were in no danger of being devoured by this particular predator. Its long, scaly arms stretched out, and Ginny stepped into them. The limbs wrapped around her, and she found herself crushed against the surprisingly warm scales. She pressed her cheek against the leathery surface as she heard the flapping of wings and her feet lifted off the ground.

She held her breath as her heart and stomach suddenly felt like they were trying to switch places as the dragon soared higher and then dipped down. Her eyes shut tight as terror seeped into her veins. Thankfully, Sybil's dragon quickly found the perfect cruising altitude, and they moved forward at a steadier pace. Instead of thinking of what was below, she concentrated on the fact that she was *flying*.

Cracking one eye open, she turned her head and looked up. The sky was a perfect blue, and the puffy white clouds were so close she could probably hold her arms out and touch them. It was like being in a plane, but so much better. The wind rushed around her, reminding her of skydiving in New Zealand, except she wasn't falling. It was exhilarating, and in this moment, she could forget all her troubles.

After what seemed like an eternity, they dipped low and

began their descent. She plastered her body tighter against the dragon's chest, holding her breath until she heard a loud thump and felt the jolt as the massive creature landed.

Her feet touched the ground, and the dragon's grip loosened. The fact that she could stand up straight without falling over was a miracle, as her knees were like jelly. But at least they were finally on solid ground, and she didn't even see the ocean as they flew. However, the thought that they were surrounded by the sea set her on edge.

When Christina had told her about this assignment, she'd been eager for the challenge. Even after working nonstop for half a year now, she had no plans of slowing down, not when her work was the only thing keeping her distracted.

Heck, she had even been looking forward to visiting a new country. But that was before her research told her she would be living on an archipelago. The name Northern Isles should have given her a clue.

"Gosh, I really needed that." Sybil, now fully transformed and dressed, exclaimed. "I don't get to do much flying these days with my duties, plus Aleksei's being overprotective with me being pregnant and all."

"Oh, I didn't realize," Ginny said. "Congratulations."

"Thanks. Now, c'mon, let's head inside." They had landed on a huge balcony, and Sybil led her through the double doors that led into what Ginny assumed was Helgeskar Palace.

"I'm back," Sybil announced. "And I brought our guest." Stepping aside, she let Ginny in.

Now or never. Ginny put on her most confident air, hopefully to mask the maelstrom of emotions inside her. "Woohoo, that was fun!" she blustered. "Reminds me of skydiving, with less falling. Thanks for the ride, Sybil. We should do it again sometime."

"Sure," Sybil chuckled.

"Are you all right? No trouble during your trip?" A tall, handsome man with dark blond hair strode forward, making his way toward Sybil. While he looked harmless in his formal suit, Ginny's lioness cowed back, as it could tell he was the biggest and most dominant creature in the room. *So, this was the dragon king.* Intimidating was a mild word to describe him.

The king placed a hand on Sybil's shoulder. "Sit down, *lyubimaya moya*. You've had a long flight."

"I'm fine, Aleksei, stop fussing," she said, then glanced behind him. "Poppy, you accepted the job, I hope?"

Across what looked like the living room of a plush apartment was a brawny giant of a man and a small, pretty woman —Poppy—who nodded. "Uh, yes ... but if you don't mind my asking, what is this about?"

"Oh, right." Sybil gestured to Ginny. "Everyone, this is Ginny. She's from the Blackstone Shifter Protection Agency."

"You're the undercover agent?" the brawny giant asked. He was even bigger than the king, probably seven feet tall, with shoulders like rocks.

Ugh, of course. She should be used to the reaction by now, but it still irked her when people underestimated her because she was female. "Well, I won't be undercover for much longer if you shout it out like that." She marched over to him, hands on her hips. "Or do you think that just because I'm a woman, I can't find your mole? I've been doing this for years now, and I've never had my cover blown. Not even my family knows about my job." She could feel this man—dragon shifter—sizing her up, but she wasn't going to be intimidated.

"Apologies, I did not mean to imply that you were not capable." He turned to the king. "But, Your Majesty, I do not understand what Poppy has to do with this."

"Remember how we were trying to find a suitable position for the undercover agent to take without arousing any suspicion? After much discussion, Sybil and I figured it out: She's going to replace Poppy as Alric's nanny."

"It's perfect, when you think about it," Queen Sybil said. "Poppy is our current nanny," the queen explained to Ginny. "With her taking the teaching position, we'll have reason to train someone new. And that means Ginny will be able to move around the palace and amongst the staff without any suspicion."

"That makes sense," Poppy added. "No one really pays any attention to me, unless I'm with the prince."

"Of course, Poppy will stay to do her duties and pretend to train you," Queen Sybil added.

"That's great! Because I don't know shit about babies," Ginny chortled. "But don't worry, I shouldn't take too long. If you have a traitor in your midst here, then we can't waste any time. I'll sniff him out for you, lickety-split." She gave herself a week to solve this case. *Ten days, tops*.

"It's settled then," the king said. "Rorik, please inform the rest of the guard of Ginny's presence so they can assist her in any way possible."

"Or just tell 'em to stay outta my way," she snorted. "I work better alone." And it was better that way. Working alone meant she could make decisions on the fly without having to consult a partner.

And if she was alone, no one else could get hurt.

After saying their goodbyes and the couple left the room, the king turned to Ginny. "I hope you are up to the task."

"I'll do my best, Your Majesty."

Sybil clapped her hands together. "Oh, sorry, I was so excited, I didn't introduce you properly." She cleared her throat. "Aleksei, this is Ginny Russel. Ginny, this is my husband and mate, His Majesty, King Aleksei of the Northern Isles."

"Your Majesty." She bowed her head in deference. "An honor to meet you." That's what you said to royalty, right? She'd never met any king or queen in her life—well, not real ones anyway. She was pretty sure that guy with dreadlocks on that beach in Thailand wasn't really royalty, even though he proclaimed himself king of the Phi Phi islands and invited her back to his palace–hut made of coconut palms.

"Ginny is actually from Blackstone and a friend of the family," Sybil continued. "You were in Jason and Matthew's graduating class, weren't you, Ginny?"

"My younger brother Gabriel was," she corrected. "I was in the year ahead."

"Ah, right," Sybil said.

"Ms. Russel, thank you for coming on such short notice," King Aleksei said. "If there is anything we can do to assist your investigation, do let us know."

"Thank you, Your Majesty."

"But first, we must make the necessary preparations to keep your identity a secret."

"I've arranged for your apartments in the staff wing of the palace. It's not fancy, I'm afraid," Sybil said.

"I don't need to stay in a five-star hotel. I'm sure it's fine. Besides, it'll help me blend in better."

"You can use this day to get settled in," King Aleksei said. "I'll arrange for you to meet with the rest of the Dragon Guard first thing tomorrow."

"Dragon Guard?" she asked.

"They're kinda like our Secret Service," Sybil explained. "The man who was here with Poppy was their captain, Rorik."

"Oh right." *Oops. Maybe I should have been nicer to him if he was the head of security.*

"Let me call on one of them to escort you to your rooms," King Aleksei said. "Excuse me." He turned around and faced the windows.

"I'm going to call our head housekeeper to make sure everything's ready for you. Have a seat." Sybil led her to the living area, then walked over to the console table and picked up the phone. "This won't take too long."

"Awesome." Ginny dropped her backpack on the floor and plopped down on the plush couch.

Seconds later, the door opened, and a figure appeared in the entryway. "King Aleksei, I'm here."

Wow, that was fast. Ginny glanced behind her. The king didn't even move an inch from where he stood. How did he call this guy?

When the newcomer stepped inside, his gaze immediately landed on her. "Oh, hello," he greeted, a grin spreading over his face.

Oh, brother. She knew that look in his eyes, and she was *not* in the mood. Her lioness, on the other hand, eyed him warily, sensing another big predator in the room. *You're going to have to get used to that*, she told her animal. This was a land of dragons, after all.

He stalked over to her, his tall, lean body moving languidly like a cat. "I think I recognize you."

"You do, do you?" She crossed her arms over her chest and stared up at him. He was cute, she gave him that, though blond pretty boys weren't her usual type. Not that she had time to entertain any type these days.

"Uh-huh." He stared right back at her, amber eyes twinkling with amusement. "You look like my next girlfriend."

She burst out laughing because there was no way that was happening. "Oh my God, did you practice that in the mirror or something? Hmmm, I'd give you ... four out of ten for effort."

To her surprise, her reaction didn't offend or anger him, and instead, he chuckled. "All right then, let me try again." He cleared his throat. "What's your sign, baby?"

She rolled her eyes. "Dead End."

"Niklas!" Sybil admonished as she put the phone down. "Stop pestering Ginny."

"Er, sorry, Your Majesty." He grinned at her again. "I have more where that came from."

"I don't want to know where those came from," she replied drolly, which earned her another laugh from Niklas.

"Well—Your Majesty." His face turned serious, and he bowed deeply.

King Aleksei walked up to them. "Niklas, this is Ginny Russel. She's the undercover agent The Agency sent to us to investigate the mole."

"Heya," she greeted.

The corners of his mouth quirked up as if he was trying

to stop himself from making some kind of smart remark. "Er, welcome, Ms. Russel. Let me know how I can be of service." The audacious man actually *winked* at her.

King Aleksei sent him a warning look. "If you don't mind, Niklas."

"Of course, Your Majesty. Right this way, Ms. Russel."

The queen looked at Niklas, one brow quirking up. He laughed and then bent down to pick up her backpack.

"Great." Ginny got to her feet. "I can carry that myself, thank you."

"Nah, it's fine." He waved her away. "C'mon, let's go."

He led her out of the suite, stopping briefly to nod at the statue standing right outside the door. A quick glance back told her that was no statue—but rather, another dragon shifter. He stood eerily still, steely eyes forward and jaw set. Something about him set her lioness on edge, but in a different way. Like it knew there was something not quite right about that other man.

"Don't worry about Stein," Niklas said. "That's just how he is. So," he glanced at her. "You're going to be the new nanny, huh?"

"I—wait a minute." She stopped and looked at him, then lowered her voice. "How did you know? I thought they didn't decide what my role would be until the previous nanny accepted her new job."

"The king told me," he said matter-of-factly.

"When?"

"He—oh!" He snapped his fingers. "I forgot, you're not from around here. As dragons of the same species, His Majesty and I can communicate via telepathy."

"Oh, no way? Really?" *Huh.* She'd never heard of any other kind of shifter having that ability.

"Yeah." He waggled his eyebrows at her and leaned forward. "Wanna know what's on my mind?"

"Oh, please." She placed a hand on his chest and pushed him away. "I don't think there's enough bleach in the world to clean my brain from the depraved thoughts lurking in there."

"I like you," he chuckled. "All right, all right, I'll stop. But first ..." He took a sniff of the air. "Hmmm ... lioness, right?"

"Yes. How did you know?" Most shifters could narrow down another shifter's animal to species, but not exact animal.

"My first girlfriend was a lioness," he said. "Not an experience I'd care to repeat. You guys are vindictive."

"Only if you deserve it," she shot back. "And I'm guessing you did."

"Probably." He flashed her a boyish grin then cocked his head. "C'mon, let's keep going."

She followed him down the long, luxuriously decorated hallway, then down a set of stairs. The palace must be huge because it took them another fifteen minutes of walking before they reached what she deduced was the staff wing of the palace. It was located on the ground floor past the kitchens, and the corridors here were more utilitarian and modest. Niklas seemed to know almost everyone and greeted them as they passed by, then led her into one of the offices where he introduced her to the head housekeeper, a middle-aged woman named Mrs. Anna Larsen.

"The nannies usually stay closer to the royal apartments for convenience, but Her Majesty told me that you would be staying in the staff wing until you fully transition into your position," Mrs. Larsen said.

"I should get going," Niklas said. "But Their Majesties requested that I give you a tour of the palace. Let's meet at the main foyer at five, if that's okay?"

She took her backpack from him. "Sounds great. See you, Niklas."

"Can't wait." He winked at her, then turned on his heel and walked in the opposite direction.

"Come this way, Ms. Russel," Mrs. Larsen said. "I'll show you to your room."

They headed down a long hallway, then stopped at the fourth door on the left. "Here you go, Ms. Russel. It's an en suite, so you should have everything you need, and the staff dining room is open twenty-four hours a day. You are welcome to eat as much as you like, plus you're free to make your own meals as well with the ingredients we stock in the pantry. If you need anything, just let me know."

"Thank you, Mrs. Larsen."

"Welcome to Helgeskar Palace." With a nod, she left.

"Alrighty then." Ginny squared her shoulders and walked inside. "Huh." The room was larger and more comfortable than she'd imagined for staff housing. There was a double bed in the corner, a large window with a view of the outside, a desk, flatscreen TV, and wardrobe. Setting her bag down on the floor, she walked over to the bed and sat down, then lay back.

She let out a long sigh. *Another day, another mission.* But this is what she signed up for, after all. It was bright and sunny outside, but despite the traveling and jet lag, she wasn't tired. She was a shifter, after all, and didn't need as much rest as normal humans. And she didn't sleep. *Not anymore.* Not when the darkness of sleep only brought on nightmares she'd sooner forget.

Getting up, she reached for her backpack. She had a couple of hours before she had to meet Niklas, so she needed to get to work. Unpack, reach out to HQ, then figure out how to hunt for a traitor who aided in the assassination of a king. *Easy peasy.*

———

"... and you're doing well so far?" Christina Lennox asked, her voice tinny through the small speakers of the beat-up laptop. "No problems?"

"Yup, all good so far." Ginny had to wait until it was morning in Colorado to call her boss via video chat, which was around four o'clock in the afternoon, Northern Isles local time. "The king said he'll arrange for me to meet his security team tomorrow and give me a more comprehensive view of the situation." She wished it was sooner, but she supposed one more night couldn't hurt.

"Excellent."

"I'll find this mole lickety-split, don't you worry." This wasn't just any normal case, after all, and not just because the dragons were one of The Agency's most powerful allies. This was personal for Christina, as Sybil was her sister-in-law.

"I know you will, otherwise I wouldn't have assigned this case to you," Christina said. "Thanks for hopping right on it."

"Just have my next assignment ready."

Christina's brows drew together. "About that ... Ginny,

don't you think it's time for a break? You've been working nonstop. Maybe you should slow down."

Ginny stiffened. "I don't need a break."

"That's what you keep saying." Christina's expression became worried. "It's been almost six months since Malta. I know it's been tough, but Kristos—"

"I said, I don't need a break," she snapped. "Sorry, I have to go meet someone soon. Bye, Christina, I'll update you as soon as I wrap things up here." She quickly slammed the laptop lid down and shut her eyes tight. Her chest tightened as if her lungs were collapsing in. Like they did *that* day, when they were filling with saltwater.

It was *everywhere*. Around her. Over her head. Smothering her like a cloak and—

Her lioness growled, knocking her out of the memory, and she could breathe again.

It had felt so real. Like it was happening again. She raked her hands through her hair, her hands still shaking.

Can't dwell on it. Need to forget. She forbade herself from thinking about that incident. It was ancient history, and she didn't need to remember anything about it.

Except Kristos.

When was the last time anyone mentioned that name around her? Or when she'd last heard it aloud?

His funeral, probably.

An ache in her chest bloomed, and her lioness mewled in a comforting manner. Counting to ten, she unclenched her jaw. *It's fine. I'm fine,* she told her animal. Her eyes darted to the clock on the bedside. "Shit!" It was five minutes to five, and she still had to find her way through the maze-like corridors of the palace and out to the main foyer. How long had she been in a daze?

Dashing out of the room, she did her best to retrace her steps out of the staff wing. But once she reached the main palace, everything looked the same. *Did we turn left or right at the painting of the guy riding a horse? Or was it the other guy on the horse?* Damn it, she was already late.

Unsure what else to do, she turned the next corner. However, she bumped into someone rushing in the other direction, sending her scrambling backwards. "Oh shit! I'm sorry!" She steadied herself. "My bad! I wasn't looking—" Ginny blinked and found herself staring into familiar amber eyes. "I ..." She gasped. *Niklas?*

Mine, her lioness roared.

And something big and fierce shrieked it right back.

Niklas's mouth parted, but nothing came out. He just stood there, amber gaze boring into her.

No, he couldn't be—

But her lioness repeated it again. *Mine.*

Niklas was her mate.

A surge of panic rose up in her. And this time, she let her flight response take over. Using her shifter speed, she ran past him, then turned into the first hallway on the right, then into the next. When she decided she was far enough away, she slowed her pace, but kept on walking.

Her heart beat like mad in her chest, threatening to escape. How could Niklas be her mate? They'd met this morning and her animal didn't say anything. Was it a delayed response?

Not every shifter had a mate. In fact, many shifter couples had successful marriages even without the mating bond, like her parents. But when her brother Gabriel had met his mate Temperance, he said that he knew right away, the moment he looked into her eyes.

Maybe I'm too broken.

Her animal shook her head. *Mine*, it repeated.

Oh God. A mate? Her? It couldn't be. She didn't need a mate right now. Or ever. Certainly not a dragon. Plus, she could never live here. Or in any one place. It would drive her mad. She needed her freedom to roam and travel.

Okay, calm down, she told herself. Maybe Niklas didn't want a mate either. Sure, he was flirty and all, but she could tell he was a player, with all those cheesy lines. Plus, he looked about as shocked as she had been.

Taking a deep, cleansing breath, she straightened herself and turned around. In her mad dash to get away from Niklas, she had somehow found herself in a familiar hallway. She'd definitely seen that statue of the man playing the flute this morning. *And that rug with the blue squiggles.* All she had to do was turn right at the end and—

"Ah-ha!" she exclaimed when she saw the long winding staircase that led to the staff apartments. At least now she could go back to her room and figure out what to do.

"Ginny?"

She stopped short at the sound of the familiar voice behind her. *Shit.* "Hey, Niklas," she began. "We should probably talk."

"Talk?"

Pursing her lips together, she turned around to face him. "Yeah. About what happened."

"What happened?"

She frowned. "You know. I—" *Wait a minute.* Narrowing

her gaze, she peered up at his face. Those amber eyes peered back at her and ...

Nothing.

Huh?

Not a peep from her lioness nor from his dragon.

What the hell?

"Ginny?" He waved a hand in front of her face. "What's going on? You okay? Do you need a minute?"

More like a lifetime. "Um, no, I'm fine. I just ... got a little lost."

"Oh." He scratched at this chin. "Yeah, when you didn't show up, I figured you must have taken a wrong turn or something. Do you want to do the tour another time? We could just grab dinner."

"What? No, I'm great. Fine. Dandy." She blew out an annoyed breath. Wasn't he going to say anything about what happened earlier?

"Oh cool. All right," he began. "Why don't I start by orienting you so you can find your bearings?"

"That sounds great." Well, if he wasn't going to say anything, she wasn't going to either. Besides, what was she supposed to tell him? *Sorry I freaked out, but I hallucinated you were my mate.*

Relief poured through her. No, the last thing she needed was a freaking dragon mate. Her animal, on the other hand, sat in the corner and pouted.

Ugh, weirdo. Maybe being out here was affecting her shifter side. In any case, that was another reason to finish this mission quickly and get the hell out of the Northern Isles.

CHAPTER 2

hat in Odin's name just happened?

Well, Gideon *knew* what happened. His dragon had screamed it at him, after all.

Mine.

The woman was his mate.

But who was she? Did he conjure her up in his mind? Was he going insane?

A perfunctory sniff in the air told him that, no, she had definitely been real. And now her delicious scent imprinted in his brain.

His dragon nudged at him, as if saying, *go after her, idiot!*

Oh, right.

The shock that coursed through him had rooted him to the spot, making him unable to move, transfixed by the vision before him—gorgeous face, lush pink mouth parted, blue eyes opened wide. Apparently, her reaction was the complete opposite, and in a flash, she was gone.

A mate. Gods, there was only one—no, two—other people he knew who'd found their mates. Mates were already rare, after all, and aside from the king and Rorik, no other dragon in the Northern Isles had found theirs. He'd been happy for them, even encouraged the captain of the Dragon Guard to pursue Poppy. However, Gideon never really thought he'd ever meet his own mate.

But she was here! His dragon rejoiced at the idea and—

A cold, dreaded feeling washed over him.

Never fall in love, Gideon. It's not worth it.

Of all the memories he had of his dearly departed father, that was the one that left a lasting impression.

But this was different, right? She was his mate, the one fate deemed to be his destiny. His king had found happiness in the queen, and so did Rorik with Poppy. Why couldn't he?

"Pardon me." Someone from behind cleared their throat.

"Apologies." He turned and nodded at the steward carrying a silver tray, then stepped aside.

How long had been standing there, staring into space? Too long, it seemed. Shaking his head, he managed to dislodge the jumbled thoughts of the past and made his legs move. Where was he going again?

Oh right, where else but the library.

As the resident information specialist for the Dragon Guard, Gideon spent a lot of time doing research in Helgeskar Palace's library. Sure, he also had his duties to perform as part of the guard, but he preferred the solitude of being surrounded by books or working in front of his computer. Originally, his twin brother, Niklas, had been the one recruited to the Dragon Guard, but when the then-King Harald found out his talent with technology, he gave Gideon special permission to leave the Northern Isles to get his degree in computer science and cybersecurity at CalTech.

When he finished his studies and returned, Gideon was able to put his knowledge to good use by building the country's cybersecurity infrastructure, as well as modernizing the systems within the palace and government offices.

Lately, however, the current king relied on him for his research skills. Truthfully, Gideon had never been happier, poring through ancient texts for clues, especially since his work could possibly unlock one of the mysteries they'd been trying to solve—how to undo the spell of a nefarious magical artifact called The Wand of Aristaeum. Their enemies, The Knights of Aristaeum, attacked the Northern Isles and used The Wand to take away then-King Harald's dragon. The former captain of the guard, Thoralf, had to leave his post and go on a quest to find a cure for The Wand.

However, that had been over two years ago, and it seemed they were no closer to finding a solution, at least not until a few weeks ago when the current king and his family had been attacked.

Truthfully, Gideon had blamed himself for all this. After all, despite the time and research he'd devoted these past two years, he'd still come up with nothing. However, he swore an oath to protect his king, and he doubled-up on research, hoping they could find a cure. Between that *and* another research project that had inadvertently landed on his lap, he was stretched thin, but this was his job and the main reason he joined the Dragon Guard.

And now, of course, his dragon scratched at him, wanting him to find this woman who was apparently their mate. Was she part of the staff? Surely, he would have noticed her before. And from what he'd heard of her accent, she sounded American. Was she a new hire?

One thing at a time, he told himself as he entered the library and sat down at the big desk in the middle of the room. There was so much work to be done, now more than ever. So many people counting on him.

Gideon picked up the book he had left on the table last night. The gilded title on the front read *History of the Dragon Families of the Northern Isles* in old Nordgensprak. He had taken this volume out of the archives as part of his research for the *other* project dropped on his lap.

Opening the book, he scanned the chapter where he left off. *In the twelfth century, the Houses came together for a trial regarding the murder of Aslaug by the hand of....*

Gideon read through about five paragraphs of the dry tome before realizing that he hadn't absorbed a word of it. *Great.* He lowered his head in defeat, then banged it against the table. This was going to be a long evening.

As it turned out, Gideon's evening did not get any better. His dragon kept insisting he scour every inch of the palace to find their mate. That sounded rather unreasonable, plus he had so much work to do, so he ignored his animal and continued his research.

After three hours, when he failed to absorb any of the text, he went back to his apartment. Of course, even while attempting to relax or sleep, his dragon would not leave him in peace. While shifters didn't need a lot of rest, tossing and turning in bed until sunrise because his dragon was having a temper tantrum was not the best way to spend the night, and by the time morning came, Gideon was thoroughly irritated and cranky.

Fine, he told his dragon. *You win.* He would search for this mystery woman today, if only so his animal would leave him alone.

His dragon let out a long, relieved sigh, then did a little happy dance.

Damned thing.

Gideon rose from his bed, got ready for the day, and after a quick breakfast, headed outside. He crept out quietly, head bowed, hoping not to run into anyone, especially not the other person who lived on this floor.

"Hey, Gideon, wait up!"

No such luck.

Turning around, he saw his twin coming out of his apartment. This was truly one of the few times he wished he and his brother didn't live in each other's pockets. Normally, he didn't mind, of course. They were twins, after all. Growing up, they'd always done everything together, and after their father's death when they were just nine years old, they truly only had each other. The longest they'd been separated was when Gideon was in California and even then, after a year, Niklas had missed him so much he decided to enroll in CalTech just so they could be together.

This morning, however, Gideon was not in the mood for his brother's antics, not when he had a pressing matter to attend to. "Niklas," he grumbled in greeting.

"Bro, I—hey, what's with the long face so early in the day? Not a good look for you. I should know," he chortled.

"It's nothing."

"But—"

"I said, it's nothing," he snapped.

Niklas raised his palms up. "All right, all right. Who pissed in your cornflakes this morning? Sheesh. I—wait! Where are you going?"

"To work." He turned his back on Niklas, hoping to avoid any more questions.

"Work? But we have a meeting with the king in five minutes."

"Meeting?" He whirled around. "What meeting?"

Niklas rubbed at his eyes. "The one Rorik called for last night. Didn't he tell you?"

"No, he didn't."

Niklas glanced around, then switched to their mental link. *Were you out of range?*

As dragons of the same species, he and the rest of the Dragon Guard could communicate via metal telepathy, but there was a limit to the range, though usually they could reach each other anywhere within the palace. But with his dragon in a sour mood last night, it might have prevented Gideon from hearing any message. *Where are we meeting?*

Royal apartments. Everyone's going to be there. "C'mon," he said, jogging a few steps ahead of him. "We're already late."

His dragon protested, but Gideon pushed it away. Duty calls, after all. Following his brother, they quickly made their way to the king and queen's private residences. Seeing as neither Rorik nor Stein stood guard outside, that meant they were already inside. Niklas pushed the door and barged in, Gideon following behind him.

"... but shouldn't we start with—"

"Sorry!" Niklas interrupted.

"Apologies, Your Majesties." Gideon bowed his head.

"You're late," Rorik admonished.

Gideon blew out a breath before lifting his head. "It won't happen—"

Mine.

"—again?"

His heart threatened to escape his chest as he locked eyes with her. His *mate.*

"What the hell?" she exclaimed. "There's *two* of you?"

Mine, his dragon repeated.

Gideon could only stare, drinking in the sight of her. Gods, she was even lovelier than he remembered. She sat on the couch nearest the window, the sun streaming in sent the red highlights in her strawberry blonde locks gleaming. Her creamy skin was marred only by a smattering of freckles across the bridge of her nose. And those eyes; they reminded him of flying on a clear morning and being surrounded by miles and miles of blue sky.

"Ginny," King Aleksei began. "You've already met Niklas yesterday. This is his brother, Gideon, who is also one of my Dragon Guard."

She gulped audibly, then turned her gaze to Niklas. "You didn't tell me you had a *twin* brother."

"You didn't ask," Niklas shot back. "But people say I'm the more charming and handsome one."

Blood rushed to Gideon's head. "You know her?" he barked at Niklas. When everyone's heads snapped toward him, he cleared his throat. "I mean ... you've met before?"

"Yeah." His brother shrugged. "Ginny arrived yesterday, and the king and queen asked me to give her a tour of the palace last night, then we got dinner with the rest of the staff."

"You forgot the part after where you literally lost your shirt to me while playing strip poker," she pointed out, her eyes twinkling with amusement.

"You're a godsdamned shark, Russel." Niklas shot her a dirty look. "Where'd you learn to play like that?"

"From the Sherpas on the way to Everest Base camp," she said cryptically.

"*Strip poker?*" It took every ounce of Gideon's strength to hold his dragon back as it lunged for his brother. Niklas played strip poker with his *mate*? It boiled his blood to think about what his brother might have seen.

"Can we please get on with our meeting?" Rorik said, rubbing the bridge of his nose with his thumb and forefinger.

"Er, sorry," Niklas said sheepishly. "Please, proceed."

King Aleksei blew out a breath. "Now that everyone is here, let's get this meeting started. The Shifter Protection Agency sent Ginny here to find our mole. She'll be working undercover as our new nanny-in-training, but aside from myself, the queen and Poppy, only the five of you know her real identity."

Gideon glanced at his mate—Ginny—who quickly averted her gaze. *So, the Shifter Protection Agency sent her.* He recalled the king telling them about this agent, but he didn't say they were sending a woman. No wonder he hadn't seen her before yesterday.

"I ask that you assist her," the king continued. "It's imperative we find the traitor among us as soon as possible."

"Of course," Rorik said. "Ms. Russel, how can we help you?"

"Ginny, please. Ms. Russel was my mother." She gave a half-snort, half-laugh that Gideon couldn't help but find adorable. "I'd like to get started right away, so maybe you all could walk me through what happened in Venice? I've read the reports, but I'd like to hear it firsthand."

"Niklas was there with us," King Aleksei began. "Why don't you start?"

Anxiety flashed across his brother's face, so fleeting that no one noticed except Gideon. How could he not, as Niklas had nearly lost his life that night? Dread, too, pooled in Gideon's stomach at the memory of that call from Rorik telling him his brother had been wounded badly. Frankly, he wasn't sure what he would have done if Niklas hadn't survived.

The atmosphere in the room turned serious as Niklas spoke. "I was assigned to escort Their Majesties that night to a dinner and ball hosted by the mayor of Venice. But the queen had been feeling fatigued from the entire trip, so it was already decided beforehand that she would make her excuses at the ball and leave after dinner."

"Who knew about this?" Ginny asked.

"Most of the delegation were told, including myself," Rorik answered. He took out a piece of paper from his pocket and handed it to her. "Here is a complete list of the delegation for the tour."

"Thanks," she said, taking it. "And then what happened?"

Niklas continued. "After dinner, things went according to plan and we returned to the hotel at around nine thirty. I entered the suite first. My eyes had barely adjusted when those men came out of nowhere and they stabbed me in the chest with a knife. Immediately, I felt weak and collapsed. My body felt like it was on fire, and then I passed out."

"There were three of them," King Aleksei said. "They had a magical artifact on them—a wand. They pointed it at me, and then it was like shackles had been placed all over my body. I could not move or call on my dragon." A perturbed look flashed across the king's face. "It was as if the wand had locked my animal away." He shook his head. "They were about to stab me, and if Sybil had not been able to get away and come back to rescue me, who knows what could have happened?"

Ginny pursed her lips. "You're sure no one else could have known you were coming back early? Couldn't they have been waiting in the suite earlier?"

"The evening nanny, Ingrid, came out to the living room around eight thirty, then went back into the nursery at nine," Rorik explained. "She would have seen anyone hiding then. I also spoke with the security team at the hotel. It seems someone had hacked into their CCTV feed at around ten past nine and fed their monitors looped footage so they didn't show anything out of the ordinary."

"Hmmm." Ginny's nose twitched. "Sounds like perfect timing."

"Exactly," Rorik added. "This was planned, and they knew when Their Majesties would be returning."

She stood up. "I'll get to work, then, Your Majesty. By the way, from this point on, it's best if you all treat me like any other palace staff. I wouldn't want to arouse any suspicion and send our mole into hiding. If I have anything to share with you all, I'll let His Majesty know." The warning tone in her voice was subtle, but unmistakable: Don't get in her way.

"If you'll excuse me." Her gaze briefly flickered over the room, but carefully avoided Gideon. Then she disappeared through the door.

And just like that, she was gone again.

Gideon let out the breath he didn't realize he'd been holding. The urge to run after her was strong, but he kept it in check. His dragon, on the other hand, reared its head, screaming at him to chase after their mate.

"Do you really think she'll find the mole, Your Majesty?" Rorik asked the king. "Not that I don't trust your judgement."

She is an outsider, Stein, who stood in the corner and remained a quiet observer throughout the meeting, said through their mental link. *How can we trust her?*

"Christina assured me, she's the best agent for the job," King Aleksei said. "But I understand if you all have your reservations. Take any necessary precautions you need."

"We will assist her with her investigation, but also stay abreast of her activities," Rorik said. "Niklas, you seem to be getting along with her. Keep an eye on her."

"Me?" Niklas asked, mouth agape.

"*Him?*" Gideon said at the same time, the words flying out of his mouth before he could stop it. His dragon lashed its tail in protest.

Rorik's eyebrow shot up. "Is there a problem, you two?"

"None," Gideon added quickly. "None at all."

"Aww geez," Niklas scrubbed a hand down his face. "She's gonna be trouble, I just know it."

"Never seen you back away from a female before," King Aleksei joked.

"You don't know what she's like," he groaned. "She's a

lioness. Those feline chicks are ten pounds of crazy in a five-pound bag."

Apparently, his brother had been cozying up to his mate this entire time and had come close enough to identity what her animal was. An ugly, hot feeling crept into his chest, then coiled tight.

"Gideon, you okay?" Niklas waved a hand at his face.

"I'm fine."

"Are you sure—"

"Yes." He stood up. "If that's all, I should go back to my duties and continue my research."

"How's that going by the way?" King Aleksei asked. "Did you find out anything else about either wand?" Right after the attack, they had deduced that the wand that had been used in the Venice attack was related to or perhaps a precursor of The Wand that had taken away Prince Harald's dragon.

"I'm working on it, Your Majesty."

"And how about the missing Dragon Guard?" Rorik asked.

"Missing?" King Aleksei frowned. "Who's missing?"

Oh Freya, how could he have forgotten?

Recently, King Aleksei had given them an additional assignment—search for his long-lost uncle who may or may not be alive. About sixty years ago, the infant Grand Duke Aleksandr of Zaratena had perished during a revolution that ultimately destroyed the country, but apparently, he might have escaped with the help of a Dragon Guard sent by Aleksei's grandfather. A witness had come forward a few months back claiming to have seen a dragon flying overhead somewhere in the Baltic region. However, in his search, Gideon found no record of any Dragon Guard sent to Zaratena.

Gideon updated the king and the rest of the team on his findings. "I've gone back sixty years, and I haven't found anything, at least not in our archives. I've reached out to all the dragon families to ask if they know of anyone in their houses who was sent abroad, but so far, I haven't had any positive replies. I also plan to contact all the retired Dragon Guard. One or two who served around the year Zaratena fell might still be around."

"Hmmm, that is strange indeed," the king said. "Surely someone would have written it down somewhere. Nothing from the Dragon Guard records either, Rorik?"

"No, those were the first things Gideon pored through." The captain scratched at his beard. "I shall ask my father if he knows anything about this supposed Dragon Guard. It's before his time, but still, he may have heard talks or rumors."

"Excellent," His Majesty said. "Thank you everyone for coming this morning. Now, I have a meeting with the transportation minister in twenty minutes, so I must go."

All the Dragon Guard bowed as the king made his way out, Stein following behind like a shadow.

"We've certainly got our work cut out for us," Niklas said. "Any chance those new recruits will be coming on board soon?"

"Don't remind me," Rorik said. "None of them pass Stein's impossibly high standards."

"We're gonna need the help," Niklas said. "With the royal family growing and Thoralf still being away."

Gideon didn't need the reminder of the failure of their

former captain—which he partly attributed to himself. "I should get going as well."

"What?" Niklas's face fell. "Oh, wait, Gideon!" He placed a hand on his shoulder. "Bro, I wasn't implying—"

"It's fine." He shrugged his brother's hand aside, then walked away. When he stepped out into the hallway, a sudden feeling of guilt coiled uncomfortably in his belly. He didn't mean to be so short with Niklas, but the reminder that none of the information he dug up over the last two years had helped Thoralf, nor brought him any closer to finding a cure for their former king, irked Gideon. And compounded by the fact that his own brother had been flirting with Ginny this entire time and was now assigned to look after her made his gut twist in jealousy.

Oh Freya, what would happen if Niklas knew the truth? But Gideon already knew how his twin would react. Niklas, unfortunately, was one of those people who was in love with being in love and constantly searched for the perfect woman to make him happy. If he ever found out Ginny was his mate, he'd push Gideon into claiming and bonding with her as soon as possible.

His dragon nodded its head and agreed.

For Thor's sake, we don't even know anything about her.

That didn't bother his dragon, of course, because all it knew was that this woman was their destiny.

Destiny? he sneered. When he entered the room, his entire being fixed on her, yet she didn't even flinch or look at him. And she ran away from him yesterday. Did he forget that fact? Then she did it again today, without a word or second glance. Like he was *nothing* to her.

His dragon let out a protesting roar, one so loud it left his ears ringing. However, he pushed his animal away, and instead, allowed the seething anger building up in him take over instead. If she didn't want him, then fine. He didn't want her either.

Never fall in love, Gideon.

He would heed those words *and* the lesson of his parent's disastrous marriage, lest he end up a broken man like his father.

CHAPTER 3

Ginny's heart raced with no signs of slowing down, even as she left the royal apartments. Her mouth was dry as the desert, and though her knees felt like rubber bands, she forced herself to keep walking.

Why was this happening to her? Here, of all places?

Mine, her lioness pined. *Mine.*

She thought her lioness had gone crazy—hell, that *she'd* gone crazy, imagining Niklas was her mate. But it wasn't Niklas her animal had recognized. It was his twin. *Gideon.*

Even saying the name in her head made her lioness purr in delight ... as well as other parts of her.

Fuck, the man was *hot*. When that six and a half feet of pure maleness strode into the room, her temperature shot up. Those bright amber eyes blazed like fire the moment they landed on her. That lock of light blond hair over his forehead made her want to reach out and brush it off. Or run her fingers through his scalp and make him moan.

She couldn't quite understand it. Niklas and Gideon were two identical looking men. Yet one didn't stir up

37

anything more than brotherly emotions, while the other could drench her panties with just one broody look. But she supposed fate did whatever it damned well pleased, even if it meant messing up someone's life.

At least he didn't rat her out.

Ginny told herself that was a good thing and only confirmed exactly what she thought: He didn't want a mate either. He was Niklas's brother, after all, and that man was a damned born lady magnet. Sure, he'd eased up on her last night, but he teased and flirted with every woman that came within six feet of him. And of course, every single one of them just about ate it all up because Niklas was handsome, affable, and could charm the pants off anyone.

Forget about Gideon, she told herself and her lioness. Before her animal could protest, she shoved it away, determined to ignore its mewls and roars. *I need to finish this case and move on.*

Speaking of this case, she had work to do. Last night's social activities actually gave her an idea of where to begin, but also reminded her that she had to keep her identity under wraps. Already, some staff had given her suspicious looks, so she knew she had to make her backstory convincing, which is why she was now headed to Sybil's office.

With Poppy on leave today, the queen had decided to bring Prince Alric into work instead of handing him off to another nanny. Ginny hadn't yet met the little rug rat, and since her role would be that of the nanny-in-training, she supposed she should at least meet her "charge."

"Good morning," she said to the receptionist outside Sybil's office. "I'm Ginny, the new nanny. I'm here to see the queen."

"One moment," the young woman said, then picked up a phone. "Your Majesty? Miss Ginny is here to see you ... ah yes, of course." She put the phone down. "Please, go right ahead."

"Thanks." Entering the office, she saw Sybil sitting behind the desk, an adorable toddler squirming on her lap.

"Oh, Ginny, hey. Nice of you to stop by," Sybil greeted and waved her over. "Come in."

"Hey, Sybil—er, good morning, Your Majesty." Not wanting to slip accidentally when they were among other people, Ginny had decided it would be best for her to take on her role and address Sybil as any employee would. "I thought maybe we should work on my cover today, so no one gets suspicious."

Sybil got up and circled around her desk. "Of course. I guess I should introduce you to you to my son. This is Prince Alric."

"Hello, cutie," she greeted. "I mean, Your Highness."

The prince stared warily at her, then reached out to grab a lock of her hair and tugged.

"Alric!" Sybil admonished. "Sorry about that."

"No worries," she said, then pried his fingers open to release her hair. "You're a strong one, aren't you?" Most shifter children didn't start going through the change until they were about three or four, but Ginny could already sense the presence of an animal inside the prince. "May I?" She held her arms out.

"You don't really have to take care of him, you know," Sybil said.

Ginny lowered her voice. "This is just in case. Besides,

unless we're sure no one is around, we should stick to the story."

"Oh. Right." She handed the prince to her. "There you go."

Ginny took the child and settled him into her arms. Prince Alric seemed unsure, his blue-green eyes looking up curiously at her.

"Do you plan to have your own kids someday?" Sybil asked.

"What? Oh." She bounced Alric up and down, making him giggle. "Um, yeah." It sounded like the right thing to say, but to be perfectly honest, she wasn't sure.

Growing up, Ginny had never been one of those girls who played with baby dolls or dreamed of having kids of her own. At best, she felt ... ambivalent about offspring. For one thing, powerful lion prides like hers treated marriage and children like a business arrangement. Her own parents had their marriage arranged by their prides, though they insisted that it wasn't quite as ruthless as it sounded. They had been devoted to each other until the day they died together in that plane crash a decade ago, and with six kids, it was fairly obvious Howard and Geraldine Russel couldn't keep their hands off each other.

But there was no way Ginny would let her current Alpha and eldest sister Genevieve arrange a marriage for her. Her brother Gabriel narrowly escaped that fate, and Ginny figured with him being out of Gen's reach, her sister would be gunning for her to settle down with a nice, boring scion of whichever lion pride they needed an alliance with.

A knock on the door jolted her out of her thoughts.

"Come in," Sybil called.

Ginny's heart stopped for a moment as a familiar face popped in through the doorway. But, when her lioness didn't make a peep, she relaxed.

"Your Majesty," Niklas greeted as he stepped inside. "Ah, there you are," he said to Ginny. "I thought I'd find you here."

"You were looking for me? Why?"

"Oh, nothing. Wanted to check in and see how you were getting on with your ... job."

"Fine, I guess?" She cocked her head at Alric. "I mean ... here I am. Just doing my job."

"I meant the other job."

Oh. Her real job. "Let's not talk about that here," she said in a quiet voice. Until the mole was found, she had to be careful about not blowing her cover.

"All right then, why don't we go somewhere else?" Niklas offered.

"Excuse me?"

"What an excellent idea." Sybil clapped her hands together. "I actually have to jump into a conference call. If you wouldn't mind, maybe you could just take Alric outside for twenty minutes? He's already been changed and fed, and if you take him around in his stroller, I'm sure he'll fall asleep."

"And I'll join you," Niklas offered. "It's my job to watch out for the prince, after all."

"All right." Having people see her with the prince could only sell her cover better. "Let's get you strapped in, Your Highness."

After securing Prince Alric to his stroller and packing up his diaper bag with the necessities, Ginny and Niklas left the office. He guided her toward the elevators, then out through a side door that led into the gardens, allowing her to exit first as she pushed the stroller ahead of the dragon shifter. When they were far away enough from the castle, Niklas sidled up beside her.

"So, do you have any suspects yet?" he asked casually.

She halted, then turned to him, eyes narrowing. "Rorik sent you to meddle into my investigation, didn't he?" Oh, she could tell the Dragon Guard captain did not trust her.

"Who, me?"

"Please," she snorted. "Asking me about my suspects? You're about as subtle as a hurricane. If it wasn't clear from what I said during the meeting, then let me use simpler words: Leave me alone so I can do my job."

"Hey, c'mon now." He held his hands up in defeat. "We're on the same side here. I only want to help."

"You can help by getting out of my way." She would not let him hover over her during this investigation. It was unnerving enough having to look at him and see Gideon's face all the time. "I don't need anyone holding my hand. I'm a professional."

"Let's be realistic here," he began. "You're an outsider. Of course Rorik doesn't trust you, no one does. He just wants to know what's going on. Just throw me a bone now and then, and I'll keep him off your back, okay?"

She eyed him suspiciously. "But you promise not to interfere?"

"Promise. Now, tell me what's going on in that pretty little head of yours. What's your plan? You have a list of suspects, right? Maybe I can help you narrow it down since I know most of them."

Ginny bit her lip, placed her hands on the stroller handle,

then continued to push it along the path. Focusing her ears, she could hear Prince Alric's even breathing, indicating that he had indeed fallen asleep.

She thought about the situation for a moment. It wouldn't hurt to keep the captain informed, plus, if Niklas could provide additional information and insight that could speed up her investigation, it would ensure she left here as soon as possible.

"All right then." Slipping one hand into her jeans pocket, she took out the list Rorik had given her earlier today. "So, there were ... twenty-three members of the delegation. Who were these people? What were their jobs?"

Niklas thought for a moment. "I believe there were five high-ranking ministers, ten members of the diplomatic corps, and six palace staff to attend to the royal family's personal needs. Oh, and Rorik and me."

"Okay, we can narrow it down by eliminating a few people. You, of course."

"Whew, thank the gods," he said with a grin.

She smirked at him. "And Rorik. What about Poppy? She's new, right?" While the king and queen had trusted her with Ginny's real identity, she didn't have a good reason to eliminate the nanny as a suspect yet.

"Yeah, but she'd never betray Rorik. She's his mate."

The word made her stumble forward, but thankfully, the stroller prevented her from falling flat on her face. "Oh. Right."

"So, do you believe in mates?"

She could feel his stare boring into her, as if he was waiting for her to react. "Sure."

"You do?" He sounded surprised.

"My brother found his mate, and they're getting married in a few weeks. Who else?"

He thought for a moment. "The diplomatic corps actually left after Rome, since we were mostly doing social events in Venice. So, none of them would have been around when the queen decided to cut the evening short."

"Great. That's ten people off the list. For now anyway, but I can circle back to them." She could not leave any stone unturned after all. "I was thinking of starting with the palace staff, since they're the most accessible to me right now. Who would have been physically closest to the king and queen and spent the most time around them and able to overhear any private conversations?"

"Probably Marte and Karl, the queen's personal maid and the king's valet." He wrinkled his nose. "But you can probably cross Marte out. She's, like, eighty years old and doesn't speak a word of English."

"Hmmm, I suppose that makes sense. We'll put a pin on her for now. Now tell me about Karl."

"You met him last night, he was the guy who stormed off when he kept losing."

"Oh, him." She recalled the brash young man who declared a woman couldn't beat him at poker. "He does have a huge a chip on his shoulder. So, three more people." Glancing at the list, she read off their names and corresponding titles. "Ingrid the night nanny, the queen's secretary Melina Gunnarson, and the king's aide-de-camp Jonas Alderman."

"How would you start investigating any suspects you didn't eliminate?" he asked.

"First thing I'd have to figure out is motive. In my experience, there are a couple of reasons that could drive a person to betrayal. Greed, fear, jealousy, or power to name a few."

"Interesting," Niklas said. "How are you going to find that out?"

"I'll send all these names off to The Agency for background checks. That'll take a day or two. Meanwhile, I need to snoop around their personal stuff. Karl and Ingrid live in the staff wing, right?"

"Yeah. But Melina and Jonas have their own homes outside the palace."

"All right, I'll start with Karl and Ingrid."

Niklas scratched at his chin. "Ingrid'll start her shift at eight so you can have all night to sneak into her room. There's an event with the agricultural minister tonight, so Karl will be occupied between six and seven o'clock. That's probably the best chance you'll get today, since the staff wing will be nearly empty while everyone's getting ready for the dinner."

"Excellent. I'll keep that in mind."

"Having me around isn't so bad, is it?" Niklas asked smugly.

She smirked at him. "Fine. I guess you're pretty useful."

"Why don't we get together later and go through the rest of that list. Maybe I can be of more use to you."

Ginny narrowed her eyes at him. It sounded like a good idea, but why did she feel as if there was some kind of ulterior motive behind his offer. Still, in the short span of their conversation, she'd already eliminated one possible suspect and found opportunities to investigate two people. "All right then."

"Great, I'll be done with my duties around five fifteen. Let's meet in the library at five thirty. I can contact Stein through our mental link, and he'll let me know when Karl is with the king."

"Sounds like a plan. But why the library? Why don't we meet in my room or your place?"

"Ooh, my place, eh?" Niklas wagged his eyebrows in a suggestive manner. "Guess that means you want to see my etchings?"

"Get your mind out of the gutter, lizard breath. Fine. The library it is."

"It's a date." He winked at her. "Now, let me escort you and the prince back to the queen, then I'll head out."

Checking on the prince, she saw his eyelids being to flutter. "All right, let's go back."

For the rest of the day, Ginny stayed with Sybil and Prince Alric. It actually worked out as she looked after the prince whenever Sybil had to step out or go on a call. When the queen had a free moment, she watched Alric, and Ginny caught up with her own work. The first thing she did of course was send the delegation list to The Agency so they could dig into their backgrounds.

"You're a natural with him," Sybil commented as she watched them play on the carpeted floor.

Ginny chased after the rambunctious prince as he dashed toward one of the planters in the corner, catching him by the waist before he could knock it over. "You know, taking care of a kid isn't as hard as it looks. It's kinda like watching over a drunk friend." She tossed Alric up, making him giggle as he pulled on her hair. "Hey, watch it, kid!"

Sybil chuckled as she got up from her desk. "I guess he sometimes does remind me of my friend Kate when she's had too much to drink. Here, let me." Taking him from Ginny, she perched Alric on her hip and kissed his nose. "C'mon, sweetie. Say goodbye to Ginny. It's almost time for you to go," she reminded her, nodding at the clock on the wall, which indicated it was five twenty-five.

"Oh right. I'll see you tomorrow, Your Highness." She ruffled Alric's hair.

"Good luck," Sybil whispered.

She bowed her head. "Your Majesty."

Ginny left the offices and headed straight for the library. Thankfully, Niklas had given her precise directions and soon enough, she found it. Entering through the heavy wooden doors, she glanced around the humongous room with rows and rows of shelves, all stuffed with books. As she walked inside, she ran her hands along the wooden shelves and spines, the distinct smell of paper and old leather tickled her nose, reminding her of the Old Library in Trinity College.

"Hello."

She stopped, her head whipping in the direction of the voice. It came from the middle of the room, where a dark-haired young boy sat at one of the huge oak desks. He looked up, studying her with onyx eyes.

"Er, hi," she greeted back. The kid was probably about ... well, she didn't know anything about children, so she wasn't sure how old he was supposed to be. But there was something about him that piqued her interest. Her lioness perked up and sniffed the air. "Oh." He was a shifter. Feline, too, from what she could tell.

"What are you?" He seemed so pure and wholesome with no trace of malice in his question.

"Lioness."

"I'm a cheetah."

"Cool." She could sense his animal's curiosity, and her own lioness, too, wanted a closer look. Walking over to him, she pulled up the chair next to him and sat down. "What's your name, kid?"

"Wesley. Wesley Baxter. And you are?"

"Ginny." She extended her hand, which he shook. "Nice to meet ya. What are you doing by yourself? Shouldn't you be with your parents?"

"My mum and her mate are going out to dinner tonight since his dad's visiting. But I asked if I could just stay and read." He glanced down at the open book in front of him. "But I didn't want to be home alone, so I thought I'd come here and wait for my friend."

"Oh, I'm waiting for someone too. He's supposed to help me. Would you mind if I stayed here with you?"

"No, I don't mind." He closed the book. "You're American, aren't you? Are you visiting your friend? How did you get here?"

"Wow, you ask a lot of questions, kid. How old are you?"

"Nine," he said. "Well? Are you going to answer my questions?"

"Yes, I'm American. And I'm here to replace the prince's nanny."

"Oh right. That's my mum."

"Poppy's your mom?" *Huh.* She thought Poppy was human. He must have gotten his cheetah from his father then.

"She told us last night about her new job." He cocked his head to the side. "I've never met a lioness shifter before. Or any other type of shifter, except my dad and the dragons here. We lived in London, and there weren't many of us in the city. Have you met a lot shifters?"

"Tons. My home town was full of them," she said. "And I grew up with four older sisters and a younger brother."

His eyes grew wide. "You have five siblings?"

She chuckled. "Yeah. You should count yourself lucky." Growing up under the shadow of her sisters had not been easy.

"I wouldn't mind having brothers or sisters," he said. "I know it would make my mum and Rorik happy."

Her heart clenched at his pure guilelessness. "I'm sure you'd make a great big brother."

He leaned toward her and sniffed. "You smell nice."

"Uh, thanks?" Again, nothing but pure innocence from him. "You're not so bad yourself."

"My cheetah thinks—oh, hey, Gideon."

Ginny went still at the sound of the name. Slowly, she turned her head toward the library entrance.

Mine, her lion mewled.

His amber eyes widened in surprise, but a cool mask quickly slipped over his face. "Wesley," he greeted back. "What are you doing here?"

"Mum and Rorik and Niels went out to dinner, but I wanted to stay and finish the latest *Adventures of Halfdan the Mighty* translation you lent me." Wesley glanced over at Ginny. "This is Ginny. She's going to replace my mum as Prince Alric's nanny."

"We've met," he stated, but didn't look at her or acknowledge her in any other way. "I have some work to do. If you'll excuse me."

She watched him turn and leave without another word or glance. This time, her lioness cocked its head in confusion. *What in the—*

A tightness gripped her chest. Gideon was ignoring her.

"Hmph." Well, what did she expect him to do? Get down on one knee and declare his true love? He'd all but pretended she didn't exist her during the meeting this morning.

"Are you all right, Ginny?" Wesley asked. "Is your friend coming?"

"Me? Uh, yeah, I'm fine. And ..." She checked the grandfather clock behind them. "He's late." It was five forty-five and Niklas was nowhere to be seen. They wouldn't even have time to discuss the list before she had to leave. According to him, she only had between six and seven tonight to snoop around Karl's room, and she still needed the dragon shifter to keep tabs on the valet. If Niklas didn't show up, that meant she'd have to take her chances and go it alone.

"You said your friend was going to help you with something?"

"Yeah ... a problem I'm trying to solve. He's probably just got caught up in other stuff." *Where the hell are you, Niklas?*

"If your friend is late, then maybe Gideon can help."

"He seems ... occupied." Ask *him?* Over her dead body. Her lioness, on the other hand, whipped its tail and let out a snarl, not liking that Gideon ignored them.

"Gideon's nice. He always has time for me," Wesley said. "C'mon, let's go ask him."

Ginny allowed the boy to grab onto her hand and pull her

along. Her animal seemed ready to scratch at her if she even attempted to resist.

"Gideon," Wesley called. He sniffed the air and then turned into one of the many rows of shelves. "Gideon, there you are."

Ginny bit her lip at the sight of Gideon's tall and muscled form leaning against a shelf, open book in one hand, aquiline nose pointed down. That single lock of hair fell over his forehead again, but it was the pure look of concentration on his face that arrested her. As if nothing else in the world existed or was as important than what he was reading. Her lion purred, and for some reason, she longed to have him look at her that way.

"What is it?" Bright amber eyes looked up from over the edge of the book. He didn't move a muscle, as if he couldn't even be bothered to expend any energy to giving her any attention.

"Gideon, Ginny needs help to solve a problem."

"She does, does she?" His gaze lowered back to the book.

"Yeah, she's waiting for her friend, but I don't think he's going to show up." Wesley drew closer to him and tugged at his free hand. "Can you help her?"

"I'm very busy, Wesley. Sorry, I don't have time to help your ... friend."

He didn't sound very sorry. In fact, he sounded downright unpleasant right now. And goddammit, she couldn't help the way her stomach clenched and her chest contracted at his chilly manner. "It's fine. I'm good waiting by myself."

Wesley's lips pursed. "But Gideon, you're always helping people. Like how you're doing research to help find the cure for The Wand or looking for the lost prince—"

"And how am I supposed to do of all that and help her too?" Gideon snapped.

Wesley's eyes grew large as saucers. "I-I-I ..." he stammered, his lower lip trembling. "I'm sorry to have bothered you." Backing away slowly, he turned, then dashed away.

Gideon's expression turned from mild shock to surprise to regret in the span of half a second. "Wesley!" he called, but the boy didn't stop. "Godsdammit." He snapped the book shut and scrubbed a hand down his face.

"Wow, way to go, asshole! I hope you're proud of yourself." Her lioness roared in fury, which surprised Ginny as she was suddenly feeling protective vibes for the kid.

"I didn't mean—"

She held up a hand, cutting him off. "Save it!" Pivoting on her heel, she strode off before she said or did anything she might regret later. Or maybe she wouldn't regret it, not after seeing Wesley's reaction. The boy obviously looked up to Gideon, and the dragon shifter acted like a jerk to him. It was one thing for him to give her cold shoulder, but Wesley had done nothing wrong.

"Fuck!" she cursed as she glanced at the grandfather clock. Five minutes to six, and no sign of Niklas. She supposed she could wait until tomorrow or find another opportunity to sneak into Karl's room, but the sooner she could get in there, then the sooner she'd be able to either eliminate him from her list or move him up to suspect number one. Then she could put this case to rest and leave this place. Rushing out of the library, she straightened her shoulders. Well, she was used to working solo. Tonight would be no different.

CHAPTER 4

Gideon felt like dirt. No, he felt lower than dirt. Wait, was there anything lower that dirt? Well, whatever it was, that was the only way he could describe how he was feeling right now.

He'd been in a terrible mood the whole day, but that was no excuse. His duties today had him patrolling around the palace grounds, leaving him too much time to think and stew about Ginny's rejection. Because no matter how many times he told himself he didn't need a mate or want to fall in love, his dragon kept disagreeing with him.

And now, he'd not only pissed her off, but he'd acted like a total jerk to his friend for no good reason. Despite his maturity, he knew Wesley was a sensitive kid. When he first moved to the Northern Isles, he had no other friend, and Gideon couldn't help but see himself in the boy. He, too, preferred the company of books to other children his age, and he never quite became popular or outgoing like Niklas.

"Mother Frigga." He scrubbed a hand down his face and put the book back into the shelf. The look of pure anger from

Ginny made his chest contract. His dragon roared at him for upsetting their mate. He wanted to go after her, but first, he had to apologize to Wesley.

He rushed toward the exit, but immediately collided into Niklas, who was on his way inside.

"Whoa!" Niklas stepped back and steadied himself. "Bro, where are you off to in a rush?"

"I have to find Wesley." He tried to sidestep his twin, but Niklas moved in the same direction, effectively blocking him. "I don't have time for this." What if Wesley was so upset, he ran away again? He'd never forgive himself.

"Wesley?" He peered behind Gideon, into the library. "Where's Ginny?"

"I ... uh, she ran off."

"Ran off? Why?"

Gideon swallowed and quickly explained to Niklas the events of five minutes ago. "So if you don't mind, I'll just—"

"Are you fucking kidding me right now?" Niklas exploded. "I send her here so you could have some alone time with her and you piss her off like that? And you were a dick to the kid too?"

He groaned. "I know I was—wait, what do you mean 'send her here'?"

Niklas crossed his arms over his chest and glared at him. "Do you think I'm an idiot, Gideon? She's yours, right? Your mate."

"How the hell did you know? Did you hear my dragon through our mental link?" It had happened to him with Rorik, which was why he was careful about keeping his link shut this morning during the meeting.

"Oh please, you can't hide it from me. Call it twin's gut

intuition." Niklas patted his stomach. "And you were about as subtle as an elephant stampede at the meeting, acting weird around her and your dragon nearly ripping my head off. Even Stein noticed and asked me what was going on."

"Stein?" He couldn't believe even the stolid Dragon Guard noticed.

"Bro, I'm happy for you!" Niklas slapped him on the shoulder. "A mate? You're so lucky. But also, good luck with that." He chuckled. "She's a handful. So, what's your game plan to claim her?"

"Claim her?" He frowned. "I—"

"Oh no. No, no!" Niklas grabbed him by the shoulders with both hands. "Nuh-uh. Not gonna happen."

"You didn't even let me finish what I was about to say."

"I don't have to. I already know you're going to say something stupid like you're not going to bond with her." His grip tightened. "Please, please tell me I'm wrong."

Gideon huffed and turned away. "You don't understand."

"Seriously?" Niklas threw his hands up. "You're going to pull this crap? You don't think that out of everyone in the entire world, I understand most of all?"

The hurt look on his twin's face made Gideon kick himself mentally. Of course Niklas would understand. He'd gone through that same hellish experience, after all.

"Look," Niklas began, his shoulders relaxing. "I get it. Watching Dad spiral like that ... it messed me up too. But not every woman is like Meryl."

His stomach dropped to his knees at the mention of ... that woman. Gideon couldn't even think of calling her *Mother*. Not after what she did to their father. His chest clenched even tighter, making it hard to breathe. "She doesn't want me. Barely looked at me." Just like Meryl. It had been over two decades ago, but he'd never forget that day. The day their mother walked out on them without so much as a backward glance. Like they were *nothing* to her.

"That's bullshit. She's your mate and she wants you."

"Oh yeah? You know her so well, huh?"

"Don't even try to deflect." Niklas's tone turned dead serious. "She's your mate. I don't want her that way. Now you better get your head on straight, make our ancestors and House proud, and *go after her*."

Gideon grit his teeth. His dragon scurried in circles, impatiently waiting for him to make a move. "I should see to Wesley first. In case he ran off and gets lost again." He had hurt his friend, and that was unforgivable.

"I'll take care of the kid, okay? But you should go after —shit!"

"Go after shit?"

Niklas glanced at the clock. "Shit, fuck, shit. It's later than I thought."

The face on the grandfather clock indicated it was two minutes after six o'clock. "What do you mean, later than you thought? What did you do?" Knowing his brother, Gideon could guess it wasn't something good.

"I uh, well, convinced her into meeting me here at the library at five, hoping that's she'd run into you. But to do that, I told her I'd help her with her investigation." Niklas briefly explained Ginny's plan to sneak into Karl Pederson's room. "And knowing how hell-bent she is on finding the mole, she's probably on her way now."

"On her way?" Gideon roared. "What if she gets caught?"

"Our plan was foolproof. I was even going to Cloak her. But now, I'm afraid she'll do it anyway, with or without my help."

"Damned fool." He raked his fingers through his hair. "All right, I'll go after her. You find Wesley."

"Great!" Niklas slapped him on the shoulder. "You get your mate!" His brother sounded giddy as a schoolgirl.

"Yeah, yeah." He wasn't sure about claiming Ginny, but at the very least, he had to keep her out of trouble. Well, the king did instruct all the Dragon Guard to help her out anyway they could, right?

Gideon quickly made his way to the staff wing of the palace. It was half empty, seeing as most of the palace employees were probably preparing for tonight's formal dinner, though there were still a few people milling about. He wasn't sure where Karl's room was, but he'd find it *and* Ginny, even if he had to tear the place apart.

Thankfully, he wouldn't have to do that because as soon as he turned the next corner, he saw a flash of black and strawberry blonde curls dart across the hallway. With his shifter speed, he quickly caught up to her, grabbing her by the arm and spinning her around. "Gin—"

"Jumping Jesus on a cracker!" she exclaimed as her blue gaze crashed into his. "Where have you been? You said—oh." Realization flashed on her face. "You."

Mine, his dragon roared.

Obviously, she had thought he was Niklas. "Sorry I scared you."

Her plush lips pursed together. "I don't get scared. What are you doing here?"

The disdain in her voice was unmistakable. "I want to apologize for my earlier actions. I had no excuse."

She blinked. "What?"

"I said I'm sorry. For—" The sound of footsteps just around the corner made them both freeze.

"Aw, shit! This really isn't the time. I have to get out of here before they see us," she hissed, trying to tug her arm away.

He only tightened his grip. "Don't worry, I'll take care of it." He Cloaked himself, and because he held onto her, she, too, turned invisible.

"Let go!" She struggled to free herself from him. "They're almost here!" Her other arm raised high, her fingers turning to claws as she readied to strike him.

"Stop it! Keep quiet!" Without a second thought, he pushed her against the wall, quickly catching her arm before she could rake her claws down his face. He pinned her wrist over her head and leaned down. "I said, *keep quiet*."

She sucked in a breath, then clamped her mouth shut. Her lioness yielded in submission, and despite his own objections, it sent all kinds of hot, erotic thoughts and feelings straight to his cock. Her delicious scent and her soft body against his set every nerve ending on fire. When he looked down at her, though, those blue orbs blazed with defiance, and godsdamned, that made him want to tame her even more.

Her nostrils flared as the footsteps drew near, her head turning to the source. He followed her gaze and saw Mrs. Larsen walking down the hallway toward them ... and passing along, not even giving them a second glance. Ginny's body stiffened, her face a mask of confusion.

When his shifter senses told him that Mrs. Larsen was long gone, he took a step back, but didn't release her wrist.

"What the hell?" she exclaimed. "What did you do to her?"

"I didn't do anything to her," he said. "I merely Cloaked us."

"Cloaked?"

"Turned us invisible. It's a dragon thing," he said.

"I'll be damned." She raised a hand to her face, waving it around. "I don't look ... invisible. How does it work? What do you mean dragon thing? Is it something you learn?"

"I'm not sure myself, but I imagine it's more camouflage than actual invisibility." He hadn't really thought of how it worked, but only that he could do it, like breathing or swallowing. "Seeing as dragons are the only fabled shifters left in existence, I can't say for certain only dragons can do it."

"Fabled shifters?"

"I'll explain later," he said. "But we have less than an hour before Karl comes back."

"Karl—wait, you know about that?"

"Niklas explained your plan. He, uh, sent me to help you because he got tied up with his duties." The lie made his stomach churn, but he didn't have a choice. If she knew what Niklas had cooked up, she might run away. Again. "Hold on." Using his mental link, he reached out to Stein. *Stein,* he called. *Are you outside the royal apartments?*

Yes, came the quick response.

I need your help. Is the king's valet with him?

Arrived about ten minutes ago.

Good. Let me know when he leaves.

Will do, he assured Gideon.

That was one of the things he liked about Stein. When any of his brothers-in-arms asked him for a favor, he didn't ask questions. "All right, Karl's with the king now. Stein will let me know when he leaves the royal apartments."

"Good," she said. "C'mon, his room's this way."

He followed her down the hallway, then stopped at one of the doors near the end. Reaching into her pocket, Ginny pulled out a small, black pouch then retrieved a long silver tool. She slipped it into the lock, then twisted it. Seconds later, there was a faint click, then the door opened.

"Yes," she cheered softy. "We're in." She stepped in first, and he came in behind her, gently closing the door. When he turned around, she was already at his desk, rooting through his drawers.

"What are you looking for?" he asked.

"I'm not sure ... but any kind of evidence that might lead me to a means or motive, if he is the mole." She shuffled through the papers. "Nothing much ... but these days, everyone keeps their stuff on their computer or phone." Turning to the laptop on the desk, she opened the lid. "Damn. Password protected."

"You'll never crack it," he said. "Not without the right tools and not before Karl comes back. Did you check his phone?"

"Phone? Why would he leave it in here?"

"Staff aren't allowed to have their personal phones on their person while on duty," he stated. "And certainly not while helping the king and queen in the royal apartments. Karl would have left his phone here somewhere."

"Ah, gotcha." She rooted through the rest of the drawers and checked underneath the desk but found no sign of the phone.

"I'll check the bed," he volunteered. The double bed was unmade and messy, a surprise considering the king's valet had to be organized and tidy all the time. As he drew closer, his foot kicked over an empty energy drink can. Frowning, he got down on one knee and checked underneath—and spied several more cans surrounded by dust bunnies.

A soft buzzing sound coming from somewhere on the bed caught his attention. Ginny must have heard it too, because she jumped toward it and shoved her hands under the pillows. "Ah-ha!" She waved the sleek metal phone in her hand. "There you go."

"You still can't crack the passcode," he said.

"But his notifications are on." Brows furrowing together, she looked down at the screen and swiped a finger down. "Hmmm ..." The phone continued to buzz in her hand. "Oh wow, someone's not happy."

"What is it?" He sidled up to her, leaning over to get a better look. This close, of course, he could smell that sweet scent again. "Who's blowing up his phone?"

Though the device remained locked, the notifications tab clearly showed message after message from a contact labeled as Jakob Luster.

She squinted. "What's he saying?"

The messages were in Nordgensprak. "Hmmm ... he wants to meet with Karl tomorrow at noon. And he's not asking." No, from the snippets he could read, Jakob sounded more like a man who *ordered* and not asked.

"Where are they meeting?"

He scanned the visible messages. "It just says the usual place."

She handed him the phone. "Let me know if anything else pops up. I'm gonna go through his papers again."

"Sure."

Though the messages from Jakob stopped, several notifications from various apps popped up.

Monaco Online: Karl, time's running out! Place your bets now.

Winner 888: Free chips, open the app now!

Xbet Dot Com: Earn two points per dollar!

Hmmm. Those sounded like online casinos. Scrolling through the rest of the notifications, he also found one from his bank, indicating he'd overdrawn his account.

"Yes!" Ginny grabbed something from the drawers and then shoved it closed.

"What is it?"

Walking over to him, she showed him. "Do these look familiar to you," she asked, waving various pieces of paper at him.

He peered at the sheets. "*La Reserve ... Ritz Barcelona ... Palacio del Retiro ... Cipriani Palace ...* those were the hotels the delegation booked during the tour."

"Just as I thought. That last one was in Venice, wasn't it?"

He nodded. "So, he kept some hotel stationary ... what does that prove?"

"Nothing yet, but look. He wrote addresses on them."

Gideon glanced at the hastily scrawled words. "Okay?"

"He could have been meeting someone to give them intel." She lay the notes on the desk, then took out her phone and snapped a photo.

"That's not solid proof he's the mole."

"No, but it narrows down my research." Gathering up the pieces of paper, she placed them back inside the drawers. "The Agency can cross-reference these addresses with dates of the tours and check CCTV footage in the area for any signs of Karl. And I'll have then dig into Jakob Luster too."

Huh. He never would have thought of that. His dragon huffed smugly at their mate's cleverness.

"There," she said. "Anything else on the phone?"

He glanced back at the screen. "No more new notifications."

"All right. I'll follow Karl to his meeting tomorrow at noon." She looked around. "I'm gonna keep looking around. You just stand guard and let me know if he's coming back."

"Right."

Gideon stepped aside as it was obvious she didn't want or need his assistance. She was quick, yet thorough, not to mention careful as she searched every inch of the room without disturbing anything. She also moved with a grace that had him mesmerized, like a dancing flame in a campfire. He couldn't tear his gaze away, even if he wanted to. But just like that fire, he knew he could get burned.

Gideon! Stein's frantic voice jolted him from his reverie. *Gideon, he's gone.*

What? Who's gone?

Karl. I was guarding the door, then the queen called me inside to ask for my assistance because Poppy's still not back. I watched over the prince for ten minutes, then went back to my post. Then the king came out, all dressed up and ready to leave, but Karl wasn't there. King Aleksei said he finished early and dismissed Karl.

63

"Mother Frigga!" he cursed softly. Sure enough, the door-knob began to turn. Without hesitation, he lunged for Ginny as she checked the row of shelves by the window, capturing her by the waist and Cloaking them just in time. Half a second later, Karl entered the room.

Ginny's body went stiff as a board, but made no sound. They stood silently, but Gideon could hear both their hearts pounding in their chests.

Karl walked over to his bed and plopped down, hand immediately reaching under the pillow, then frowned.

Oh shit. Gideon realized the phone was still in his hands. *Shit, shit, shit!*

The valet's nose wrinkled in confusion as he continued to search for his phone, and when he didn't find it, got up and began to pull the covers and pillows off the bed.

Ginny glanced down at his hand, rolled her eyes, then took the phone. She slid it down to the floor, then kicked it across the room, sending it skidding under the bed.

"Ah! There you are," Karl exclaimed. As soon as he crawled in, Gideon dragged Ginny to the door and by some miracle of the gods, they managed to slip out quietly.

"Let's go," she said, dragging him down the hallway. Her grip on him was ironclad, so he had no choice but to follow her. Okay, that wasn't quite true, as his dragon could easily overpower her, but he found he didn't want her warm palm to let go of his forearm just yet.

They turned down the next hallway, then she made a beeline for one of the doors on the right, then slipped inside. When the door closed, she released him.

"Whew, that was close." She blew out a breath, sending a stray lock of strawberry blonde hair that had escaped her ponytail flying. "What the heck happened? I thought he'd be gone the full hour?"

"Er, sorry about that. Stein left his post for ten minutes to help the queen, and Karl must have slipped out."

"At least we got out of there," she chuckled. "You okay there, bud? Your heart's running a mile a minute." She patted his chest. "Never been in dangerous situations before? I thought you guys were like supercharged bodyguards or something."

"I trained for combat, not espionage." But that wasn't why his heart was jackhammering against his ribs. No, it was *her*. He'd been too occupied earlier, but now, it all rushed into his brain at the same time—how he'd held her in his arms, the feel of her body pressed along his. Her scent. The sensation of her hair brushing his cheek.

Something changed in her expression, as if she could sense it too. Panic and dread, then exhilaration and relief had given way to something else in the air, something that crackled like electricity, thickening the atmosphere. He almost choked on it and from the way she sucked in a breath with difficulty, she felt it as well. The sexual energy hummed between them, ready to light up at any moment.

Her gaze dropped to his chest. He followed her eyes and realized she still had a hand on him. When she attempted to pull away, he caught her wrists and hauled her closer. His dragon let out a low, pleased rumble at the contact.

She gasped, clearly surprised by the move. And frankly, so was he. He'd never thought of himself as some kind of dominant, alpha male type. Even prided himself on being raised a proper gentleman. Sure, he didn't do relationships, but he treated all women with respect. And while he surely respected Ginny, the things he wanted to do with her right now were far from respectable.

Her lips parted in a soft pant. "Gideon."

Desire struck him deep in the gut at the sound of his name from her lips for the first time. When her lashes lowered and her lioness once again bowed in submission, an urge seized him—and he was done fighting it.

With a growl, he slid his fingers into her hair, pulling her head back so he could capture her mouth. The touch of their lips sent him into a frenzy, the need to have her taking over his mind. His tongue slid between her lips easily, and he knew from that first taste that he was completely addicted.

She moaned into his mouth, tilting her head back so he could explore her deeper. Her hands slid up his chest, shoulders, then to his surprise, her fingers thrust into the hair above his nape. He growled low when she tugged hard, the sensation going all the way to his cock. It throbbed underneath his pants, and he rubbed it against her stomach to ease the pain.

She must have felt it because she froze for a second, then groaned as she ground her body against his. Fuck, it sent his need for her spiraling, and he kissed her deeper. Their tongues clashed, teeth gnashed at each other, and the pleasure from the friction between them was pushing him near the edge. *Oh shit.*

He pulled away from her and stepped back, barely stopping himself from coming in his pants. Ginny, however, closed the distance between them, driving him backward until the back of his knees hit something. Her hands pushed at his chest until he fell back on the *bed*.

She flashed him a naughty grin before she straddled his lap, then lowered herself over him, pressing her mouth to his.

That second kiss was even better than the first, and she teased him with her tongue. When he lifted his head, her hands cupped the sides of his face to keep him still, and he acquiesced ... for now. She continued to kiss him softly and rub her sweet little body against his, and he fought the urge to lift his hips so he could feel that friction again. But when the scent of her wetness and arousal hit his nose, his control broke, and he quickly flipped their positions.

"What the—"

He silenced her protest with his mouth. How was it that each kiss was better than the last? It was mind-boggling, but the need to have her, touch her, was strong. His hand moved to the front of her tracksuit jacket. Finding the zipper, he slid it down, her scent intensifying as he exposed her neck and torso. He needed more of it, wanted to bathe in it, so he moved lower, licking and sucking at the skin on her neck, making her pulse jump.

He tugged the zipper down until the jacket split open, and his hand immediately went to her breast, cupping it through the thin T-shirt and bra she wore.

"Oh!" Her fingers thrust into his hair, tugging at the roots. "Gideon."

He slipped his fingers into the neckline, feeling her naked breast, the nipple quickly hardening against his palm. He moved his head lower, wanting to taste more of her.

Gideon.

He pulled the neckline down, exposing her lovely, firm breast. Her alabaster skin flushed prettily, the puffy pink nipple begging for his mouth.

Gideon!

"What?" That wasn't Ginny's voice calling him. No, it came from his mental link. *Stein?*

Where are you? the other Dragon Guard asked.

Damn.

"Gideon?" Ginny peered down at him, her pupils still blown up as her breath came in short pants.

"I ... er, pardon me." He scrambled off her and sat up on the edge of the bed. *What is it?*

You're needed at the dinner. Prince Harald decided to attend at the last moment.

Right. As a member of the royal family, protocol and security dictated that His Highness have his own Dragon Guard escort at official events. While Gideon very much liked the former king and would die for him, his timing was rotten. *I'll be at His Highness's apartments in five, er, ten minutes.*

He shut down the mental link and ran his hands through his hair. *Oh Freya.* Whipping his head around, he saw Ginny sit up and zip her tracksuit jacket up to her neck. "Um, sorry. Stein, er, was calling me."

She cocked her head. "Via telepathy, right?"

"You know about that?" Well, at least he didn't have to explain to her. Not that this was any less awkward.

"So, what did he want?"

He blew out a breath. "I'm needed at the dinner. Prince Harald decided to attend."

"Ah." She swung her legs over the side of the bed. "Duty calls then."

A pit formed in his stomach. He didn't want to leave her, not like this. "Ginny—"

"It's all right, you have work. And so do I." She got up, and slipped her phone out of her pocket.

He could feel her pulling away from him, that indifferent mask slipping into place, like they hadn't been all over each other in a desperate frenzy. Like those soul-searing kisses had meant nothing to her. It seemed so easy for her to switch it off. His chest tightened as he remembered the words of his father.

Don't ever fall—

Mine!

The dragon's roar was so fierce and loud, his ears rang. She, too, must have felt it because she gasped, her head snapping toward him. Her lush, swollen lips parted, and he saw the slightest tremor in her knees and sensed the soft yielding of her animal.

Her blue eyes grew wide. "Don't you dare—"

He was on her in a nanosecond, arms winding around her, mouth claiming hers. She struggled, but sighed and opened to him. *That's it*. Good girl.

When he was done drinking from her lips, he released her. "We'll talk later. I'll come by after the dinner."

"Later?" She blinked. "What do you mean ... no!"

"No?" he growled.

Her nostrils flared as she crossed her arms over her chest. "I have work to do. And I still have to search Ingrid's room."

Sensing she needed some time and space, he relented. "All right." But he wasn't going to give her too much space. "Tomorrow then."

"I—"

"Yes. Until then, sweet dreams."

"I don't sleep," she said sourly.

Before she could protest, he gave her one last, hard kiss before he turned on his heel and walked out the door.

His dragon let out a smug huff, as if saying, *I told you so.*

Yeah, yeah. But a smile tugged at the corner of his mouth.

He didn't initially come here to claim her. No, that had been the last thing on his mind. He had no plan to bond with her, not with his emotions jumbled up and the fear of what had happened to his parents lurking in his mind. But, gods-dammit, Niklas was right. Ginny belonged to *him*. That first touch of their lips burned that elemental truth into his very soul. He wasn't about to let her go or let anyone else have her.

CHAPTER 5

Ginny watched the sunrise from the window as she lay in bed. Her eyes felt dry and tired, but even if she managed to close them, sleep eluded her. Usually, after two days of no sleep at all, she would have given in to her body's demand for some rest.

Now, however, she couldn't even catch a five-minute snooze. It used to be that she fought the darkness of sleep because of the nightmares that plagued her, but this time it was different. When she closed her eyes and her mind relaxed, her thoughts would inadvertently settle on him. *Gideon.*

"Ugh."

She rolled over onto her stomach, but that made it worse because she could smell his distinct, masculine scent all over her sheets. Her thighs clenched together involuntarily and her nipples hardened, thinking of his mouth and hands on her. Those Goddamned talented mouth and hands. If he hadn't received that mental message from Stein, who knows how far they would have gone.

Her lioness pouted, as if saying, *Pretty far.*

Damned horny kitty.

It had been a mistake to kiss with him. The excitement and exhilaration of their successful mission went to her head, giving her a rush. And then he went all dominant alpha on her, and she just about creamed her panties. She considered herself a modern take-charge, sex-positive kind of gal. But with Gideon, it was as if some primal part of her had surfaced, wanting to be taken and claimed and—

"Gahh!" She shot up off the bed and scrubbed a hand down her face. Tomorrow, he said. Well, it was definitely tomorrow, but there was no way she was going to see him today. Or tomorrow or the day after that. Or ever. She would just have to avoid him as best she could while she was here and solve the case quickly.

Unfortunately, her search of Ingrid's room proved fruitless as she didn't find anything that could point to a motive or means. Like many of the people of the Northern Isles, the tour had been her first time outside the country, and a quick check of her phone—which she had left unlocked—revealed nothing except that she spent a lot of time texting with her boyfriend who owned a bakery in the capital city and sent her cute pictures of his Labrador retriever.

There was still Melina, Jonas, and Karl, of course. She'd sent off their names to The Agency. Christina assured her they'd work the background check on all of them, as well as look into what she had discovered in Karl's room. Walking over to her laptop, she opened the lid and scanned her inbox. *Ah-ha.* An email from The Agency. Clicking on the unread message, she scanned the contents. *Huh.*

Apparently, those addresses written on the hotel

stationary notes were pawn shops and their tech guys were still working on getting footage from the days he would have been there.

Why did you visit four pawn shops in three different countries, Karl?

Perhaps his contact owned or did business through those shops and used them as dead drop sites. Hopefully, The Agency could get their hands on some CCTV footage so they could find out what he did there and who he met. And then there was today's meeting with Jakob Luster. The Agency hadn't sent any info on him yet, but maybe she'd find out more when she trailed Karl today.

Not sure what else to do, she showered and got ready for the day, dressing in a casual outfit of leggings and a light sweater. Sybil hadn't mentioned any type of dress code for nannies, and she'd seen Ingrid wear something similar last night when she left for work.

She headed to the kitchen and ate breakfast. Afterward, she made her way to the royal apartments, carefully checking every corner, just in case Gideon was around. *Idiot,* she told herself. *What's he gonna do? Jump out from behind a Ming vase and maul me?*

Her lioness curled up, then showed its belly in anticipation.

Tramp.

Thankfully, when she got to the king and queen's residence, Rorik stood outside. She nodded at the captain of the Dragon Guard, then headed in. Sybil and Poppy were already in the living room with the prince, and so she told them about her plan to trail Karl at noon.

"Hmmm, I never really liked him." Sybil's silvery eyes

narrowed. "He seemed too ... squirrelly. But I can't see him committing treason."

Ginny twisted her lips. "You'll be surprised at what people can and will do with the right inducement."

"Well, then good luck with today's plan. Who else is on your list?"

"I'm still waiting for Melina and Jonas's background checks for anything that might indicate a motive before I start snooping. And since the diplomatic corps went back to the Northern Isles after Rome, that only leaves the five ministers. Do you know any of them?"

Sybil pursed her lips. "Yes, actually."

"From the look on your face, you've got an opinion about them."

"One of them, anyway." Sybil looked around, as if making sure no one else was listening. "Minister Valens. He clashed a lot with Aleksei and Prince Harald, too, when he was the king."

"Valens, huh? What's he minister of?"

"Commerce. Apparently, he wants to open up more trade and even tourism into the Northern Isles." Sybil's nose wrinkled. "Both Pappa and Aleksei have rebuffed him numerous times. Aleksei tells me that Valens's family owns the Northern Isles's biggest cargo and import goods company. Sounds like they'd benefit a lot if we did open up. And personally? I think he's a bit slimy, with that fake smile and the way he's always showing his misogyny with compliments like how I'm such a 'good' queen doing my duty by quickly producing the heir to the throne." She rolled her eyes.

"What a smarmy git," Poppy piped in.

"Ugh, I haven't met him, but I already know he's a Grade

A asshole," Ginny said distastefully. "So, he could personally benefit if Aleksei was out of the way. I'll definitely have to put him high up on the list. See what else his family company has been investing into." She took her phone out of her pocket and quickly typed off a message to The Agency to ask them to look into Valens. Her gut told her that if the minister had been counting on the assassination to succeed, he'd already be preparing for a potential trade and tourism boom.

"I'll let you know if I can think of anything else that might help. And if you need my help in any other way, just ask. Anyway, I should get going." Sybil got up from the couch, then stalked over to where Alric was playing on the carpet with Poppy and kissed her son on the forehead. "I'll see you later, let me know how it goes." She waved to them as she headed to the door.

"I will, Your Majesty."

"If you want, you can head out before noon," Poppy said as she handed Prince Alric a toy horse. "After Karl finishes assisting the king in the morning, he's usually with Mrs. Larsen helping with housekeeping and wardrobe duties."

"Thank you, that's good to know." At least now she knew where to start.

"So," Poppy began. "You've met Wesley."

"Oh, right." How could she forget about the kid? The look of hurt on his face had been genuine and tugged at her heart. "How is he? I hope he's feeling better?"

"Better? Was there something wrong with him?" Poppy's dark brows drew together. "He didn't say anything. We didn't get home from our dinner until late, but he seemed all right. Niklas was with him, and they were playing board games."

Niklas was with him? "Um, it's nothing. I just thought he seemed ... uh, shy."

Poppy's face softened. "That he is. He doesn't have a lot of close friends. Gideon was the first one he really took a shine to around here."

Her heart leapt at the sound of the name, but she ignored it.

Poppy continued. "They both love reading and books, so I'm not surprised. Of course, he talked about you the whole morning."

"He did?"

She nodded. "He was quite excited, actually. I think it's because you're a shifter. Lioness, right? I kind of looked over his shoulder and saw him searching about lions on his tablet."

Ginny chuckled. "He's a great kid."

"Don't be surprised if he starts wanting to be around you all the time." Poppy got up as Prince Alric did, following after him as he toddled toward the couch. "He does that to Gideon, but he doesn't seem to mind and genuinely seems to like Wesley."

"Er, right." She pursed her lips. It was a good thing Poppy didn't see how Gideon had treated her son last night.

"I think he has a crush on you. But you'll let him down easy, right?" Poppy asked with a grin.

"Crush?" *How adorable.* "I should be so lucky. Oomph!" Prince Alric crashed into her legs, and she caught him before he toppled over. He giggled and then grabbed a handful of her hair.

"Maybe Wesley's not the only one with a crush on you." Poppy gave her a wry grin, then sat on the couch next to her.

"Ha."

She spent the rest of the morning helping Poppy with the prince, but kept glancing at the clock, anticipation in her veins. At eleven o'clock, she bid Poppy goodbye and made her way back to the staff wing. As she casually walked by Mrs. Larsen's office, she peeked in the door. Sure enough, Karl was there, sitting in front of the desk, head bent down as he pored over receipts. Turning around, she went back to the kitchen, grabbed a plate of food and sat at a table where she wasn't completely facing the office, but could easily monitor it from the corner of her eye.

She waited, pushing at the food and pretended to play with her phone. Sure enough, fifteen minutes later, Karl came out of the office, dressed in his jacket, then walked past her.

Counting to ten, she got up and followed him as he left the staff wing. She trailed a good distance behind him, using her shifter hearing to follow the sound of his footsteps. When he disappeared through a doorway, she paused outside. When she picked up the sound of an engine revving, she rushed in.

The room was actually a parking garage filled with various vehicles. The sound of a motorcycle speeding away caught her attention. "Fuck!" Of course, he'd need to be driving some kind of vehicle to his meeting with Luster. What did she think he would do, take the bus? *Maybe I can borrow one of these cars and—*

"Ginny."

The low baritone sent a pleasant shiver down her spine, all the way to her core. Her body tensed as Gideon approached her. Fear and excitement coursed through her at the same time as she thought of last night when he strode toward her and wrapped his arms around her so assertively. Like it was his right to just touch and kiss her whenever he pleased.

"What are you doing here?" *Tomorrow*, he had said. Those words were obviously a promise he intended to keep.

"I should be asking the same of you." Bright amber eyes regarded her. "It's almost noon. Did you find out where Karl was meeting Luster?"

"Who?" *Oh, right.* Damn hormones. "Shit!" She glanced back toward the garage exit. "He just left on his bike. Are there any company pool cars or something?" There were several vehicles parked, but they all looked to be personal cars. "Never mind, I'll just hotwire one of them."

"Hey, hold on." He gripped her arm as she turned, sending another shock of desire through her. "I'll help you go after him."

She wanted to say no, but time was of the essence. "All right, where's your car?"

"Car?" His eyes twinkled with amusement. "We don't need a car. I'm right here."

"Don't need a—oh." He meant he could fly after Karl.

"You don't mind, do you?"

"Mind? Not at all. But if we're going to fly after him, we should go now."

"Agreed."

They hurried toward the exit, and as soon as they were outside, Gideon snaked his arms around her, pulling her close. "Hey!" Her body, however, melted right into his. "What—Oh!"

He shifted so fluidly and effortlessly that she didn't have

time to process it. Large, scaly arms tightened around her as her feet lifted off the ground, and soon, they were flying.

Ginny sucked in a breath as she craned her head around. Unlike Sybil, Gideon's dragon was a greenish-blue color. She wished she could see more of him, but it was difficult from this angle. Besides, they had work to do.

The dragon swooped down low, and as she focused her vision, she saw the black sport bike racing out the palace gates. They followed it down the long private driveway that led out onto the main road, then down the highway. Karl took the exit ramp with the sign for Odelia, the capital city, and soon, they approached the main city center. The bike wound through the streets before heading into an open-air parking lot.

They hovered above the lot as Karl hopped off his bike, then jogged to the cafe across the street, sitting down at one of the outside tables. Slowly, they descended, and her feet touched the cobblestone sidewalk as she felt the arms around her shrink and the scales turn to skin, the transition so smooth that his dragon's wings barely disturbed any of the trees or people around them.

"Don't worry, we're still Cloaked," he whispered, his mouth so close to her ear she could feel his hot breath.

"Thanks." She moved to get away from the circle of his arms, but he grabbed her hand and entwined their fingers. It felt oddly more intimate than when he embraced her. "Do you mind?"

"You need to keep touching me to stay invisible, remember?" He gave her a boyish grin.

"Right. C'mon then, let's go." She dragged him in the

direction of the cafe, pulling him urgently as she didn't want to miss a second of Karl and Luster's meeting.

"We're invisible, not ghosts." He pulled her back when a woman walking her dog nearly bumped into her. The woman kept walking, but her little Pomeranian, however, turned its head and growled. "And animals and other shifters can still sense us."

"Good to know."

They crossed the street and stopped a few feet away from Karl as he sat within the fenced-in area of the cafe's patio tables. Glancing around, she led them toward the wall of the building. "This should be close enough to hear them without anyone bumping into us."

"Almost time," he said, nodding across the street where a large clock hung outside what appeared to be a watchmaker's shop. The long arm on the face pointed to the last line just before the twelve. And sure enough, when the clock struck noon, another man walked into the cafe and headed straight for Karl.

Ginny sucked in a breath and leaned forward, focusing her hearing as the man—Jakob Luster, she presumed—sat across from Karl. They spoke in clipped tones, in, unfortunately, the local language.

"Want me to translate?"

She tamped down the heat building in her stomach. "Please." Christ, she sounded needy.

Gideon drew up behind her. His arm slipped around her waist and pulled her close, lining up her back with his front. "People can still hear us," he explained, his lips near her ear again.

She squirmed, but his grip stayed firm. "Can you please not—"

"Shh." His warm breath blowing into her ear turned her knees to jelly. "One sec."

Ignoring the desire flaring in her, she focused her attention on Karl and Jakob. Though she couldn't understand what they were saying, she could read their body language clearly. Luster looked calm and relaxed, leaning back in the chair, while Karl became more nervous and agitated.

"Luster's asking him where his money is," Gideon began. "He's been patient, but time's running out."

Karl leaned forward, hands wrung together.

"Karl's asking for more time. He's trying to get the money together ... but is offering him—" Gideon stopped suddenly, his body turning rigid as Karl took something out of his pocket and pushed it toward Luster.

She squinted at the small package as Luster opened it and peeked inside. His mouth curled up into a smile. "What is it?"

He blew out a breath. "According to Karl, a diamond cufflink. From King Aleksei's wardrobe."

"Holy fuck." She chomped on her bottom lip. So, Karl owed Luster money. Loan shark, probably. *Sounds like a motive.*

"Luster says this is okay for now, but he still owes him the rest." She could hear Gideon grinding his teeth together and mutter something under his breath in Nordgensprak that sounded unpleasant. "How much does he owe this man?"

Luster stood up and slipped the package into his front coat pocket, then turned and walked out of the cafe to a waiting limousine. Once the vehicle was gone, Karl got up and walked back to his bike.

"We should report him to Rorik and the king," Gideon said. "Stealing is a crime. When I was looking at his phone last night, I saw that his bank account had been overdrawn and he had several gambling apps installed."

"Gambling addict. Figures." He'd been furious when she beat him during the poker game the other night, and he'd only lost his clothes.

"But is that motive enough to commit treason against the king?" Gideon asked.

"I don't know, but Luster or someone else could easily put pressure on him. Clear his debts in exchange for a little info. He might not have realized someone was trying to kill King Aleksei. Not that that's an excuse."

"Definitely not." Anger practically radiated from Gideon. "If he did betray us, there will be no mercy for him. We should take him back now before he flees and—"

"He won't run." Her gut told her that. "Besides, unless he can fly, he can't leave the Northern Isles. Also, he doesn't know we're here. I bet he's gotten cocky, thinking he's getting away with it."

"What do you propose we do?"

"Confront him with the evidence we have when he gets back. I don't think he'll try to betray the king again, or at least he won't have a chance to. That tour was a rare chance for The Knights to strike. We've caught him red-handed, stealing from the king. That should be enough to shake him down for info on his contact. Maybe pick up Luster, too, and see if he's involved." Somehow, she didn't think so, but they should check him out just in case too.

"All right, let's go. I'll call Rorik on my phone now and let him know, then we'll meet back at the palace."

———————

The flight back was uneventful; nevertheless, Ginny had been too tense to enjoy the experience. Her lioness, however, felt only peace and calm being in the dragon's embrace. A few times, it let out a satisfied purr, which the dragon replied to with a deep rumble.

Instead of going back to the garage, the dragon maneuvered them toward the east side of the palace and landed on the same balcony Sybil used when she first brought Ginny here. Had it been only two days since she'd arrived? It seemed like a lifetime ago.

"Karl's already in the royal apartments, being interrogated by Rorik and the king." Again, Gideon's transition was so smooth and effortless that she hardly noticed the arms around her were human again. "Rorik says to come inside and remain Cloaked so we don't give you away."

"All right, let's go."

They snuck inside, and sure enough, Karl sat on a chair in the middle of the room, Rorik towering over him as King Aleksei stood off to the side, looking calm and serene.

"I'm sorry, Your Majesty!" Karl looked pleadingly toward the king. "I was ... desperate. Luster threatened not only to hurt me but my family as well if I didn't pay up."

"Gambling? Really?" Rorik said in an exasperated voice.

"I ... I can't help it. It's like a drug." Karl buried his face in his hands. "I just ... each turn I keep thinking, I'll win it back. And I usually do, but then I think, just one more bet. One more and I can change my life. My family's life. But then I lose my streak."

Rorik snorted. "So, you were desperate. Desperate enough to betray your king?"

The valet's head snapped up. "Betray the king? B-but I only took a few pieces—"

"What were you doing sneaking off to pawn shops during the tour?" Rorik's eyes began to glow. "You know you're not supposed to leave the hotel without telling me or any of the security team. I checked the logs, and there was no record of you asking for permission to leave. Don't deny it—we have evidence of you going to those places."

Ginny doubted they had the footage yet, but it was a good bluff on Rorik's part. It was obvious Karl was ready to break down and confess.

"Did you tell someone that the king and queen were coming home early from the mayor's dinner?" Rorik roared. "Answer me!"

"No!" Karl went pale. "I didn't ... I s-sold more jewelry. It was the only way ... I couldn't sell them outright here. It would have been traced back to me." He flew off the chair and got down on his knees. "Please, Your Majesty! Have mercy on me. I didn't betray you," he sobbed. "Please."

The king and Rorik looked at each other silently, then Rorik turned to where Ginny and Gideon stood. As the captain's bright green eyes focused somewhere above her head, she realized they must be speaking telepathically.

Finally, the king spoke. "Karl Pederson, you'll be taken into custody and placed in the Odelia city prison. As our justice system demands, you will go on trial and be judged by your peers."

Karl let out a pathetic cry. "I'm sorry, Your Majesty. I truly am."

The king remained stony-faced. "Take him away."

Rorik grabbed him by the elbow, hauled him to his feet, and dragged him out. Once the door slammed shut, Gideon released her.

"What do you think?" King Aleksei asked, his piercing blue-green eyes staring right at her.

Ginny thought for a moment. Karl was the perfect suspect. Opportunity and motive were there. She wanted him to be the mole so that she could close up this case and be on her way. But she had to listen to her instinct. "I'm sorry, Your Majesty. I just don't think it's him."

King Aleksei's shoulders slumped. "Neither do I. And I'm not just saying that because he's my valet and I personally selected him for the position." He shook his head. "Such a bright young man, ruined by his own weakness."

"It could still be him," Gideon said. "We can open up his phone and laptop. See if he communicated with anyone during the tour."

The king sighed. "We definitely will have to take those into evidence, but something tells me we won't find anything except more proof of his gambling addiction."

She hated to admit it, but she agreed with King Aleksei. Still, she had to be sure. "The Agency is getting CCTV footage from the pawnshops he visited. We'll be able to confirm Karl's story that he only went there to get cash for your stuff or if he met with anyone suspicious."

"Do what you must. Do you have any other suspects?"

She gritted her teeth. "I don't, Your Majesty."

"She's working as fast as she can, Your Majesty," Gideon

piped in. Though his tone was respectful, Ginny didn't miss the way his body tensed and his fists curled at his sides.

King Aleksei didn't either and raised a blond brow at the Dragon Guard. "I am not criticizing you, Ginny. I'm thankful for your help and glad you found that thieving fiend before he sold off more of the royal jewels. I'm aware you've only been here two days. Thank you for your assistance as well, Gideon."

The look that passed between them made Ginny uncomfortable. Like they were talking about her. "I should get going. The Agency might have sent me the information I need."

Without a backward glance at Gideon, she strode to the door and left the room. She barely got six feet before she heard the familiar low baritone call after her.

"Ginny! Wait."

She thought about running, but knew it would be pointless. Besides, her will and energy were slowly sapping away. "What?" she groused.

Gideon caught up to her. "Don't be too hard on yourself. Like the king said, it's only been two days. And Karl was your first suspect."

"I know that. It's fine. I should get back to work." Hunching over, she shoved her hands into her pockets. When she attempted to sidestep him, he blocked her way and reached out to tip her chin up with this finger. "Do you mind?" She glared at him.

Those amber eyes narrowed at her, filled with a genuine concern that made her stomach flip. "Are you all right? You seem tired. Is it the jet lag? Have you slept at all?"

"I told you, I don't sleep. If you'll excuse me—" She sucked in a breath when his warm hands gripped her arms.

"You need to rest."

"I'm *fine*. The king wants me to find the mole as soon as possible."

"The king wants you performing at your best, so you can do just that. Trust me. He even asked me to assist you in this matter."

"He did, did he?"

"Of course. When he found out that I had helped you track down Karl, he insisted I continue to help you." He smirked at her. "He ordered me to stay by your side and make myself available to you anytime."

A rush of giddiness zinged through her at the double meaning in his words, but she managed to tamp it down. "Ordered you, huh?"

"I'm duty-bound to do as my king commands."

His smile deepened and—*damn it!* She hadn't noticed he had dimples before. It made him look even more handsome and appealing. Her lioness, too, mewled in approval.

"Look, if you don't want to go back to your room and rest, why don't I help you get your mind off this case for an hour or two?"

She worried at her lip. "I suppose I could use a quick break."

"Whenever I need to relax, I go flying. There's nothing like being up there, feeling the wind rush around you, surrounded by clouds and blue sky. It helps me think and work out problems. C'mon, Ginny."

She really shouldn't accept his offer. *Say no.* It was the

right thing to do. They shouldn't entertain this ... thing between them, not when she had no plans of staying here.

"I know you enjoyed it. Don't deny it." He flashed her another devastatingly charming, dimple-filled smile.

"Okay." God, she hated that she loved his dimples so much. "But if you let go of me and I fall, I'm going to come back as a ghost and haunt you at the most inconvenient times."

He held his hand out. "I would never let you go, *pusen*."

The words struck something deep in her, and a sudden mix of fear and excitement nearly made her turn tail and run in the opposite direction. Her lioness, however, dug its claws into her. "All right." She took his hand, and once again, he interlaced their fingers.

He led her out of the royal apartments and the main palace, all the way outside to the front lawn. He stepped back a few feet and stretched his arms out.

The air seemed to shimmer around him as his torso and limbs began to stretch and elongate. She gasped as she realized that his clothes changed with him. No other shifter she knew did that, not even Sybil.

Gideon continued to grow and grow until a fifty-foot dragon stood in front of her. Actually, it looked more like a serpent with a long, slim body and bat-like shimmery wings. Its scales were a light blue-green and covered every inch of its snake-like body. A giant maw opened and let out a snort, then lowered its head to stare right at her.

She should have been wary; afraid even. When faced with a bigger and more dominant predator, her lioness, too, was usually cautious. But she felt none of those things, only a deep sense of calm as she stared into giant amber eyes. *Gideon's eyes.*

Reaching out, she stroked its snout, and the dragon let out a rumble. "You like that, huh?" The dragon blinked at her in agreement, then reared back and opened its arms. She backed into them without hesitation, and the scaly arms tightened around her.

She let out a scream of delight as they shot up into the sky. Below her, the palace became smaller and smaller until it all but disappeared and she could only see green underneath her and blue all around. The dragon flew through the clouds, the coldness making her shiver in delight. The rush of excitement in her veins made her forget about the world below—and everything and everyone there.

How long they'd been flying, she wasn't sure. Up here, it was as if time didn't matter at all—only the blue sky, pure white clouds, and the dragon's arms wrapped around her. She closed her eyes, letting it all sink in, and pushed away all her thoughts and worries.

When they dipped low and her stomach leapt into her chest, she quickly opened her eyes. They were now flying over a mountain range, all green and lush from the first buds of spring. When they continued to descend, she sensed they were about to land somewhere. Sure enough, the dragon hovered over a clearing before gently setting them down. The air crackled with energy as she felt him shift back.

"Your clothes change with you," she said. "How?"

He released her and stepped back. "It's another quirk of fabled shifters."

"You mentioned that word before, but I've never heard of it." She faced him. "What does it mean?"

"I'll tell you more, but you have to follow me." He held his hand out again.

"Follow you?" She glanced around. "Wait ... why did we stop here? Where are we going?"

"I brought us down here because I wanted to show you something."

"Show me ... something?" she echoed.

"Yeah." The corner of his mouth quirked up, and he rubbed the back of his head with the heel of his hand. "It's kind of ... it's a place I go if I need a break. Like if I'm stumped with my research or just need to relax." He nodded toward a line of trees up ahead. "We'll have to hike for a bit."

"Hike?" she exclaimed. "You didn't say anything about a hike. Why can't we just fly there?"

"Because it's half the fun and part of what helps me think. How about I answer any questions you have along the way?"

They were supposed to be flying, not going on a nature trek, but it wasn't like she could just walk off and go back to the palace on her own. So, she took his hand and allowed him to pull her along. Besides, he'd pricked her curiosity with all this fabled shifter business.

He led her toward the trees, through a rough path that led deeper into the forest. "Most shifters are called 'common' shifters, meaning their animals exist in the world. Like you," he began. "But fabled shifters are those whose animals don't have real-life counterparts."

"Huh." She'd never realized the distinction, but it made sense. "How many types of fabled shifters are there?"

He stopped to brush a stray lock of hair from her cheek. "As far as we know, it's just dragons now. But according to what I've read, a few centuries ago, there were others like us. Basilisks, manticores, griffins, unicorns, and a few others."

"What happened to them?"

"We don't know. They just ... died out. Probably hunted down, like the rest of our kind." A dark look passed across his face, but he turned away and continued to lead them through the trees.

"But Sybil ... why can't she change her clothes the way you do?"

"Ah, yes. Sybil and the rest of her kind—mountain dragons, that is—were banished from the Dragon Alliance a few generations ago, and according to her, they just never learned how to do it or use their mind link. It's a fascinating story, she'll tell you all about it if you ask."

"Interesting. I—ooh!" Her foot got stuck under a root, and she stumbled forward.

Gideon quickly caught her and pulled her against him, an arm winding around her waist. "I have you, *pusen*."

Her cheek pressed against the hard, muscled wall of his chest. She took in a whiff of his delicious scent, which sent her lioness into a frenzy. Lifting her head, her gaze clashed with his, and those haunting amber eyes darkened with desire. "Gideon ..."

He lowered his head, pressing his lips to hers, the kiss surprisingly gentle today, compared to yesterday's frantic make-out session. But the yearning in her didn't burn any less hot. How the hell could one man evoke such a response from her?

Mine, her lioness reminded her.

"C'mon," he murmured against her mouth. "We're nearly there."

"Nearly ... there?" she breathed. "Where?"

He flashed her a cryptic smile. "You've learned almost everything about water dragons, but there's one more special ability I want to show you." Wrapping his hand around her elbow, her motioned for her to keep moving along the trail.

"Special ability, huh?"

"Yes, something unique to dragons of my kind." He pushed aside a low tree branch and guided them through. "Here we are."

"Here? Where?"

He nodded to the path in front of them. "Go on."

She walked ahead of him, past some low bushy plants, kicking aside some branches and large rocks that blocked the way. As she pushed past the boulders, her keen hearing picked up a sound that sent her heart leaping to her throat. Her chest squeezed tight, and it was a miracle she could breathe at all when the memories rushed back into her mind, brought on by the sight of the bubbly, foamy surf crashing against the beach.

Water. So much water, slowly swallowing her up. The heavy weight pulling her down, she could barely keep her head above it. Her lungs filling up. Couldn't breathe. Chains around her ankles and then—

Something fast whipped by her, knocking her out of her nightmare. *Gideon*. He dashed toward the surf and dove right in.

Ginny opened her mouth to scream, but nothing came out. The waves continued to smash against the rocks and sand, churning like a foamy soup bubbling over. Seconds ticked by, and she realized he hadn't come back to the surface.

No!

Her chest squeezed into itself, and her heart told her to go in after him and save him. But she remained paralyzed, gripped by fear as the nightmare played like a movie in her head. Her limbs were locked into place, her feet glued to the ground, and she could only scream in her mind as she watched the treacherous seawater swallow up her mate.

Suddenly, something large burst out from the water—a large, scaled head, blue-green snake-like body, and a fluked tail. Gideon's dragon let out a screech, backflipped, then plunged back into the ocean. Ginny's heart followed the motion before landing like a heavy stone in her stomach.

The dragon slithered out of the water and began to transform until Gideon stood a few feet from her. His mouth was turned up into a grin. "What did you think—Ginny?" He dashed to her side. "Ginny? What's wrong, are you okay?"

She opened her mouth, but nothing came out.

Snap out of it!

"Ginny?"

When his hand landed on her shoulder, she shrugged it off. "Take me back."

"Take you back? But we just got here. I wanted to show you—"

"I said, *take me back!*" she cried, then kicked herself for sounding weak and freaked out. Because those feelings were starting to take over, and if she didn't get out of here, she was afraid of what she'd do in front of him. "Please."

His expression softened. "Whatever you want, *pusen.*"

The arms that enfolded her grew and turned scaly. She found herself being lifted up, and the loud whoosh around her told her they'd taken off.

The flight was fairly quick, and she spent most of it with her face pressed against the dragon's scaly hide. She found that if she focused her hearing, she could listen to its heart—Gideon's heart—beating like a steady drum. Oddly, it calmed her, and her body relaxed as the tension eased out.

Finally, they landed on solid ground. Glancing around, she recognized the front lawn of the palace where they had taken off earlier. As the dragon shrank, she considered running away so she could avoid the questions Gideon would inevitably ask. However, he shifted so fast, she barely had time to turn around.

"Ginny," he began. "Are you all right? What happened back there?"

"I'm f-fine," she insisted. "I just ... I have to work on this case, okay?"

"You don't look fine." He reached out to her, but dropped his hand when she flinched. "I'm not going to hurt you. Why are you acting like this?"

"Acting like what?" Her defenses immediately shot up. "You don't even know me!"

His expression darkened, and those amber eyes blazed. "Don't know you?" He growled. "How could you say that? You're my—" He froze as a buzzing vibration sounded from his pants pocket. Biting his lip, he took his phone out and scanned the screen. "It seems I'm needed as well."

"Duty calls," she said. "You shouldn't keep His Majesty waiting."

"Ginny ... will you at least get some rest? Maybe a nap or a full night's sleep."

"I told you, I don't sleep," she snapped. "You should go. We both have work to do." Ignoring that pleading look on his face, she turned on her heel and walked away. *Please don't follow me.* God, she needed to be alone.

The emotions churning in her felt like bile rising in her throat. The past just wouldn't let her move on. It kept a hold on her like those chains that had pulled her down into the dark depths of the ocean. She'd escaped death but continued to be haunted by the memories.

Forget about them. Don't think.

When she reached her room, she pushed them deep down and locked them away. Maybe this time they'd stay locked up. *I have a job to do.* Yes, this job provided relief from the pain and memories. That's why she couldn't stop, couldn't rest, couldn't let her guard down or even sleep or else they'd escape again.

Bracing herself on the desk, she blinked several times, then plopped down on the chair. She opened her laptop and watched her email come in. She immediately clicked on the one from The Agency's top analyst, Nepheli Kritikos.

First, Nepheli wrote that they were still working on Melina and Jonas's background check, but the next line in the email had Ginny leaping up and raising her fist in the air. "Yes!"

Just as she thought, The Valens Group of Companies were looking to acquire a failing Danish airline, as well as a fleet of cruise ships from some liquidation auction in the Bahamas. *Sounds like someone wants to cash in on a potential tourism and commercial boom in the Northern Isles,* she thought wryly.

Pushing away from the table, she paced around, gnawing on her lower lip. She would have to access Minister Valens's phone, email and personal calendars, plus computer files for any suspicious communications or evidence that he'd met with anyone on the day of the dinner. It would be easy enough to check the CCTV cameras at the hotel, so she fired a message back to Nepheli to ask her to track Valens's movements that day.

Now, how to find solid proof that Valens was the mole?

She supposed she could find out where Valens was and follow him around and wait for an opportunity to steal his phone. Or she could break into his office or work and try to look at his files or his computer. But that would all take time and research as she had no idea what kind of security measures he employed or even where his office was located.

An idea struck her. "Of course!" There was an easier way to get to Valens: Have him come to her. But for that plan to work, she would need Sybil's help.

CHAPTER 6

As Gideon watched Ginny dash back into the palace, the urge to run after her nearly overpowered him. His dragon, his gut, and his very being all screamed at him to go to her and make everything better. Truly, he would have done anything to put a smile on her face again.

What had happened back there at the beach? She'd been happy and glowing after that kiss, and the next moment, it was as if something horrific had occurred. Her face turned pale, her lips trembled, and her entire body froze. He couldn't even reach out to her lioness as it had grown agitated and freaked out. But what triggered it, and more important, what could he do so it never happened again?

Helplessness seeped into his very bones. His dragon, too, sank into despair, not knowing how to make things better for their mate.

Gideon, came Stein's voice. *Are you back?*

Yes, I'll be there in a second, he said as he headed into the palace. He'd forgotten that he was supposed to relieve Stein after lunch, as the other dragon guard had a training session with the new recruits this afternoon. He made his way to the king's office and nodded at Stein, who stood outside the threshold.

Everything all right? Stein asked.

Gideon took his post on the other side. *Yes.* He did a double take. Stein never asked him if he was all right before.

Did your mate find the mole?

Not quite— "My what?" Surprise made him say it aloud. *How did you—never mind.* Niklas and his big fat mouth. *I suppose everyone knows now.*

Asking Niklas to keep a secret is like asking a wolf to guard the henhouse. So? How goes it? With your mate? And the identity of the traitor?

Stein sounded uncharacteristically curious. Concerned, even. Not that the stone-faced Dragon Guard didn't care for anyone, but he was hardly the type to pry into someone's personal business. *We're working on it,* he answered.

Stein nodded at him and stepped forward. *I must attend to the pack of competent morons who have miraculously made it this far in the Dragon Guard training. Perhaps today I can drill more lessons into their thick heads and elevate them into capable clowns.*

Gideon mentally shook his head. Most people thought Stein was mute or just wasn't a talkative person. But he could be creative with his use of language when he wanted to be. *All right. I'll be fine here. Good luck with your trainees.*

Squaring his shoulders, he straightened his stance and placed his arms at his side as he stood guard, ever alert in case his king needed him or anyone dared threaten him.

He didn't particularly hate this duty, but today he didn't enjoy it. It gave his brain too much idle time, and his thoughts eventually drifted to Ginny and the incident at the beach. His gut clenched whenever he remembered the emptiness in her eyes and all the blood draining from her face. But why did she act that way? What had triggered that response in her? Though he tried to analyze it and replay it in his head, none of it made sense.

Gideon did his best to stay alert, at least, manage to look serious as people came in and out of the king's office. Though they'd already gone through thorough security checks before they even stepped foot in the palace, it was still his job to keep the king safe. Part of his Dragon Guard training was to scrutinize everyone who came in and out, check for unusual behavior or signs of nervousness or other indications they may be hiding something. He also had to keep his mental link open in case the king called for help.

King Aleksei did his best to keep regular hours, but it wasn't unusual for him to attend to his duties until supper-time when he dined with the queen at their apartments. Gideon was ready to leave by the time the king exited his office.

Good evening, Your Majesty, he greeted.

Gideon. The king looked at him wryly. *So ... Ginny.*

He groaned inwardly. *I was going to tell you, Your Majesty. But she and I have yet to sit down and talk about it.*

King Aleksei raised a blond brow. *And your little trip this afternoon didn't involve any talking?*

Damn. A hot flush of embarrassment crept up his cheeks.

Say no more, Gideon. The king held up a hand. *It's a private matter. I understand completely. But know I am happy that you have found the other half of your soul. Having a mate is one of the greatest gifts from the universe. I look forward to seeing the bond between you form.*

Thank you, Your Majesty. And knowing he had King Aleksei's support boosted his waning confidence.

The king cleared his throat. "The queen has just informed me that our dinner plans have changed. We are to head down to the formal dining room now as she has invited some guests to dine with us tonight. Come."

He trailed behind King Aleksei as he made his way to the first floor. When they entered the receiving area before the dining room, it was already abuzz with activity, but everyone stopped what they were doing as soon as the butler announced the arrival of His Majesty. All the guests immediately bowed or curtseyed.

"There you are," Queen Sybil said as she approached them.

"Apologies for my tardiness, *lyubimaya moya.* I had to take care of a few things."

"Of course. Thank you for indulging me in this last-minute affair. I was just ... feeling social tonight." A look passed between them, indicating they were communicating through their private mental link. "Come." She slipped her arm through her mate's. "I'm starving, and our guests are waiting."

The royal couple led everyone into the dining room and Gideon, as well as Stein, who had probably been assigned to guard the queen tonight, followed inside and took their place by the exit.

It was quite unusual for the queen to entertain at the last minute, especially such a mixed group. He recognized a few familiar faces, such as Melina Gunnarson, Jarl Solveigson and his daughter, Lady Vera, but there were a few random people as well, such as two judges and three ministers.

As they all sat down and the dinner service began, Gideon prepared himself for the long wait. These things were usually drawn out and boring, at least for whoever was on duty. When the servers came in with the first course, his dragon immediately perked up, eyes and ears on alert.

What in Thor's name was the matter?

His eyes scanned the guests, looking for any signs of danger. However, one person—a server with short, dark hair carrying a tray with plates—caught his and his dragon's attention. Something about the way she moved with a cat-like grace made it hard to look away. And when she turned to put a plate down in front of the finance minister, he realized why. The hair was different, but the face definitely belonged to Ginny.

What was she doing here?

He continued to watch her circling the table to serve the dainty-plated appetizers. His fingers curled into his palms as he fought the urge to run after her as she finished and left, but he couldn't cause a scene.

Stein, he called to his companion. *I need to leave. Just for a minute.*

Leave? You cannot leave, not while the king and queen are here.

I know, but ... it's important. It's about the investigation into the mole.

The stoic dragon guard let out a soft snort. *Fine.*

Thank you.

Quietly, he crept out of the dining room, then into the hallway before rounding the corner where the servers were using the side entrance to bring food in. He spotted Ginny as she exited. Using his shifter speed, he dashed to her, then pulled her into an empty hallway, pinning her against the wall and covering her mouth in case she screamed.

Sky blue eyes blinked at him.

"It's me." He took his hand away.

"What the hell, Gideon?" she hissed. "I'm trying to work here!"

"Why are you serving dinner?" He glanced at her short, bobbed hair. "And what are you wearing?"

"It's a wig, duh." She crossed her arms over her chest. "And I told you, I'm working. On the case to be precise."

"Who's your suspect? And what's your plan?"

"You don't have to concern yourself with that. If you'll excuse me—"

"Ginny." He gripped her arm. "Maybe I can help. Make this easier for you so you can solve the case faster."

She hesitated for a moment, but then her shoulders relaxed. "I came up with the plan to get one of my suspects here so I can steal his phone. I was going to use his wine glass and lift a print to unlock it. The queen agreed, and she thought it would be a good idea to invite the other people on my suspect list and see if I can do the same with their phones."

"Hmmm, that's not a bad idea."

"Not bad? It's brilliant! I have all the equipment ready back in my room to fake their thumbprints to open the phones."

"Yes, but how long will that take?" he pointed out. "How many phones do you plan to steal and how much time will that give you to look through each phone? Plus, you have to both remove and return the phone without their respective owners realizing what happened or they'll suspect something's wrong."

She opened her mouth, then shut it again before letting out a huff. "It's a chance I'll have to take. "

"I have a better idea."

Her expression turned skeptical. "You do?"

"Yes. I know a way you can get the data you need, take your time combing through it, and not have to worry about returning the phones."

"How?"

"Meet me back here in fifteen minutes and I'll tell you, okay?"

"I—all right." She shrugged off his hand. "This plan of yours better work."

"It will. Trust me. Now, I have to go."

Leaving her there, he made his way outside, sending a quick apology to Stein to let him know he'd be gone a little longer. He dashed to his apartment, retrieved a device from his room, and headed back to the same spot he left Ginny, arriving just in time as she rounded the corner, holding a bottle of red wine.

"Well?" she asked. "What's your plan."

"Here." He held up the device, about the size of a brick but half the thickness. "This will clone any phone within two feet. With this, you can copy the data from your suspect's cell without even having to touch them. The downside is that you have to keep it near the target for about fifteen minutes or more, depending on how much data it has."

Her jaw dropped. "Where did you get this?"

"I, uh, made it."

"You made it?"

"Er, yeah. Part of my senior thesis at CalTech."

"CalTech?" she asked incredulously. "What do you mean—"

"I'll explain later, but we're running out of time. Who are your suspects?"

"Minister Valens, Minister Ossler, and Melina Gunnarson."

He thought for a moment, thinking of the seating arrangement. "All right. Melina and Ossler shouldn't be a problem as they're next to the king and queen on either end of the table. I can talk with them through our mental link and let them know of our plan. You can pass the cloner to them and retrieve it when you're done. Valens, unfortunately, is right smack in the middle of the table."

"Damn. And he's my top suspect too."

"Wait. I believe he's seated beside Lady Vera. Perhaps if you could slip it into her purse, that might work. Just make sure you retrieve it before the end of the evening."

"All right, sounds like a plan."

"Let's go back before anyone realizes we're missing. Let me go in first and tell everyone the plan." He left her and slipped back into the dining room.

Everything okay? Stein asked as he returned to his position.

Yes. For now, anyway. Reaching out to the king and queen, he looped them and Stein into the plan. The king and queen agreed of course.

And she'll be able to retrieve the device once it's done copying Valens's phone? Stein asked, his stare fixing on Lady Vera.

I'm sure she'll manage.

Ginny returned at that moment, so Gideon settled back and watched her like a hawk as she made her way to the queen. She was so quick and her movements so graceful, he didn't even notice her pass the device to Queen Sybil, but the *got it* message he received from Her Majesty confirmed that she had done so.

When they began to serve the main course, Ginny deftly took the cloner back from the queen, then passed it to the king. Gideon tracked Ginny's movements, while counting the minutes in his head as the guests continued to enjoy their main course. The servers, unfortunately, would not be returning until after this course was finished. Ginny only returned to retrieve the device from King Aleksei as she cleared plates.

When the servers came back with the dessert course, Ginny passed behind Lady Vera, placed the dish of lingonberry sorbet in front of her, then knocked a fork off the table with her elbow.

"Pardon me, my lady," she said in Nordgensprak, then bent down and disappeared for a half a second, before popping back up. "I'll get you a new one." With that, she dashed off.

As the dinner continued, Gideon's heart pounded in his chest. Things were winding down, but there was no sign of Ginny.

Finally, the servers once again returned to serve coffee and clear the plates, but at that moment, Lady Vera decided to get up and head toward the bathrooms. Ginny arrived too late, her composure slipping for a second when she realized that Lady Vera was not in her seat and now nearing the exit. She met his gaze, eyes widening in panic.

We have to do something, Gideon said to Stein. *Quick! Stop her from leaving!*

Without hesitation, Stein stepped to the side, blocking the door as Lady Vera approached them.

She gasped as she nearly collided into the humongous Dragon Guard. "Excuse me, I—" Her lips twisted as she lifted her head and met Stein's silvery gaze. "Oh. It's *you.* Will you kindly step aside and let me out?" The sarcasm dripping from her tone was unmistakable.

Stein snorted. "Dinner is not done."

"Yes, but I need to go ... powder my nose."

"For security reasons, you must stay here," Stein stated.

"Stay here?" Lady Vera said incredulously. "Are you out of your mind? You cannot stop me from leaving."

Gideon stepped forward, sidling up beside Lady Vera. "Is something the matter, my lady?"

"This ... this *lout* says I can't leave the room because the dinner is not over!" Her violet eyes blazed as she tossed Stein a look of disdain. "I've always been able to use the facilities at any time when I dine here."

"My apologies, Lady Vera." Gideon bowed his head. Reaching over, he deftly slipped his hand into her purse and quickly found the device, then took it out and put it in his pocket. "We had some changes in security because of recent events." He lowered his voice. "I'm sure the queen has confided in you about Venice?"

"I—Yes," she huffed. "But I'm not a threat to Their Majesties."

"We are still testing out a few new protocols." He glanced

at Stein, who remained unmoving and stony-face. "Looks like we have to tell Rorik that we need to re-think the no-leaving rule during dinner, don't we, Stein?"

Stein only grunted in response.

"Why don't you let the lady through?"

He took a step aside, clearing the exit.

"Hmph." Lady Vera tossed her hair and shot Stein another murderous glance before storming off.

Whew. Gideon glanced wryly at Stein. *You really saved us there.*

He only grunted in response, though Gideon could feel how wound up Stein and his animal were. He recalled Niklas mentioning how the Jarl's daughter could provoke the normally stolid Dragon Guard. But that wasn't surprising because at one time, Lady Vera had set her cap on Aleksei and being queen herself, and when Sybil Lennox arrived, Lady Vera had treated her poorly. That was a long time ago, however, and the two women had actually become the best of friends, putting their differences aside to work together on improving the conditions at the local orphanage. Of course, Stein wasn't the forgive-and-forget type, and he probably still remembered the lady's antics and disposition toward their beloved queen.

Returning to his spot, Gideon caught Ginny's eyes as she cleared away more plates. He gave her a slight nod. Relief broke on her face, and she smiled at him, then ducked her head and continued her work.

The rest of the evening passed with no more incidents. After dinner, the king and queen invited their guests to the library for drinks and coffee. Gideon wished the night was over so he could work on the data they'd collected from the phones, but more importantly—be with Ginny again. She'd all but disappeared when they left the dining room, and he figured they didn't need as many servers here.

Finally, after what seemed like forever, the king and queen thanked their guests and announced they were retiring for the evening. Everyone graciously said their goodbyes as the royal couple headed back to their apartments, Stein and Gideon following along.

Did everything go smoothly? King Aleksei asked.

Mostly, Gideon answered. *But I have the device. Now I only need to crack the data, and we can see what Valens, Ossler, and Melina have been up to. Actually, I should go see Ginny.*

Ah yes, go and help your mate, the king said.

Queen Sybil stopped in her tracks. "Your *what?*"

King Aleksei looked at her sheepishly. "Um ... well ..."

"Ginny is your mate?" The queen looked at him. "Really?"

He pressed his lips together. "Uh. Yes, Your Majesty."

"Why didn't you say anything?" she asked, then turned to her husband. "And why didn't you tell me if you knew?"

"It wasn't my place," he answered. "And it was Niklas who told me, by the way. I'm sure he would have told you if you'd seen him."

"Oh, Gideon, I'm so happy for you." The queen beamed at him. "And Ginny's an amazing person." She clapped her hands together. "That means she'll stay, right? Oh, it'll be so nice to have someone from Blackstone here. Have you bonded yet?"

"I'm, uh, working on it, Your Majesty." He bowed to the couple and then nodded to Stein. "If you'll excuse me." Oh, he really was going to kill Niklas, twin be damned. He supposed Rorik and possibly Poppy knew too. It's not that he was ashamed, but right now, things were still muddy between him and Ginny. They hadn't even said anything out loud to each other about the whole mate thing. Perhaps when this whole mole business was over and done with, they could focus on their mating, which was all the more reason for him to help her out.

Seeing as they didn't agree on a place to meet, he headed back toward the dining room. However, he was only halfway there when he spotted her rounding the corner, still dressed in the server's uniform, though she no longer wore that ridiculous wig.

"Ginny!" he called. "Over here."

"Did you get it?" she asked, dashing to him. "Where is it?"

"I got it." He patted his pocket.

"Great, let me have it and—"

"And what?" He cocked his head at her. "Do you happen to have the equipment to read the data?"

Her mouth twisted. "I could send it back to HQ, and I'm sure they'll figure it out."

"Which could take a few days," he pointed out.

She crossed her arms over her chest. "You want something for it then, don't you?"

"Yes."

"Well? What is it? What do you want?"

"I want you to get some rest." He gently touched her shoulder. "You look absolutely exhausted. Like you're about to fall over. You need sleep."

Her nostrils flared. "I told you, I don't—"

"Sleep. I know, I know," he sighed. "You may not need sleep, but I do. And cracking and transferring the data from all three phones could take a while. A couple of hours per phone at least." Still, he wanted to make sure she was nearby. His dragon, too, didn't want her out of their sight. "How about this: I'll get the cloner hooked up to my computer and let my software work on it. Meanwhile, you can watch over the progress while I get some sleep."

"I ... suppose that's fine. All right then."

"C'mon then." He cupped her elbow. "Let's go."

"Go where?"

"Back to my apartment."

"Your apartment?" She pulled her arm away. "You didn't say anything about going back to your place."

"Where do you think my equipment is? Now, do you want to get this data or not?"

She eyed him suspiciously. "Fine," she relented.

He led her out of the residential wing of the palace, through the winding halls until they reached the North Tower, the home of all the Dragon Guards. They took the stairs up to the second floor, which he shared with Niklas. Thankfully, his brother was on overnight duty so they wouldn't run into him. Unlocking his door, he motioned for her to go inside first.

She glanced around. "This is your place, huh?"

"Yeah, it's not much compared to the rest of the castle, but it's home." Most of the furniture came with the apartment, and he hadn't really done any decorating, but the masculine decor, dark paneled walls and plush carpeting suited him just fine. "My computer's in here." He nodded toward the hallway off to the side of the living area. He entered first and then walked over to the large computer desk with double monitors mounted on the wall behind it. After powering up the PC, he hooked up the cloning device to his CPU and sat down on the chair.

"So, CalTech, huh?" Ginny raised a brow as she strode up next to him.

"I majored in cybersecurity and computer science." He tapped on the keyboard to execute the commands that would begin the process of copying the data over to his hard drive. "It was the king—that is, the former King Harald's idea to send me there after I expressed an interest in computers. He's very forward thinking and anticipated my skills would be a good addition to the Dragon Guard."

"Huh." She leaned down, looking at one of the photos he had on his desk. "Wait, is that Niklas with you? In the graduation gown?"

He chuckled, glancing at the photo of him and Niklas on graduation day wearing matching caps and gowns. "Yeah. He got bored here, and he said he missed me. So, he asked if he could enroll too. As you know, Niklas can be very persuasive, and he joined me in California. Of course, Niklas spent most of his time partying and surfing." His mouth curled up into an involuntary smile. "How he managed to finish his degree in finance, I don't know. But he did."

"Huh." She contemplated the photo for a while, then moved to the one next to it. "Oh. Now this is adorable." Her face lit up as she grabbed the framed photo. "How old were you?"

"Eleven, I think." He knew the photograph she was looking at—it was of him and Niklas, standing outside Aumont Park, arms around each other.

"And that house—wow. Impressive."

"Ah yes, Aumont Park. The ancestral home of the House of Aumont—that's the name of our dragon family."

"It looks like a beautiful place to grow up in."

His throat tightened. "Beautiful, yes."

"Do you go back often?"

"Sometimes. Usually if there's an occasion, like for birthdays. Holidays. Of course, my aunt and uncle welcome us anytime we want to come for a visit or use the house for parties."

Her brows drew together. "Aunt and uncle?"

"Yes. Aumont Park belongs to the eldest dragon of the family. My Uncle Philip owns it now, and so my cousin Lars will inherit it." His chest tightened, but he could see the confusion on her face, so he pressed on. "We were sent to live there when my father died." It wasn't that his childhood had been terrible, but the surrounding circumstances were not good memories. He had Niklas, at least, and his aunt and uncle and cousin had treated them like their own.

"I'm sorry." She put the photo back on the table. "I lost my parents too. Plane crash."

"I'm sorry too."

"At least they were together when it happened."

He got up and gathered her in his arms. To his surprise, she relaxed against him. He didn't bother correcting her that not both of his parents were dead because he preferred not to go down this particular memory lane. Instead, he focused on the feel of her body against his and breathed in her intoxicating scent as he buried his nose in her hair.

A beep made him pull away abruptly. "It's done copying," he announced, then bent over the desk to tap on the keyboard. "All right ... the cracking software's ready to start. Whose phone did you want it to work on first?"

"Valens. He's my top suspect." She explained about what The Agency's background check had revealed about the minister's business holdings.

"All right then ..." He typed a few more commands. "This should be done in a few hours." He pushed away from the desk and motioned for her to take the chair.

"Great." She sat down. "What are you going to do?"

"Sleep." He nodded at his bed. "If you need anything, there's a kitchen in the main room stocked with the basics, but if you ring the operator on the service phone, they can bring you whatever you want. If you'll excuse me." He headed to the bathroom, closing the door behind him. He slipped his shoes and socks off, then the rest of his clothes and stepped into the shower.

After a quick wash, he dried himself with the towel hanging from the rack and put on his gray sweatpants, then went out. Ginny hadn't moved from the chair, her gaze fixed on the screen. "Everything okay?"

"Yeah, I guess." She turned her head to face him. "What's this—" Her jaw dropped, and her pretty blue eyes grew large.

"Yes?" He could hardly keep from grinning as Ginny continued to stare at his torso and chest. As a shifter and Dragon Guard, he knew his body was far fitter and toned than any human's. He never really cared about it one way or the other, but the look of lust on his mate's face made him appreciate his build. "Are you all right? Is the program still running?"

She blinked. "The *what* now?"

He grinned at her. "See something you like?"

A blush crept up into her cheeks, and she whirled back to the screen. "The program's just fine. Dandy."

Seeing Ginny all flustered and bothered put him in a lighthearted mood. Contrary to what most people thought, he wasn't serious and studious all the time. Once in a while, he had a playful streak like Niklas.

Walking toward the bed, he slipped between the covers and moved to the other end, leaving some space. "If you change your mind, there's always room for you here."

Her shoulders tensed. "I'll be fine."

"Goodnight, Ginny."

"Goodnight, Gideon."

As he lay his head on the pillow and pulled the sheets up, he kept his gaze on her. *My mate.* He still could not believe it, but here she was. Only a few feet from his bed. If he were a more devious man, he could put more effort in seducing her. That kiss from this morning, and from yesterday, only proved that she wanted him as well. And he wanted her—not just her body, but all of her.

His dragon grumbled inside him. *Mine,* it demanded.

Oh shush. We must be patient. But soon, he thought as his mind powered down and sleep began to creep into the edges of his brain. *Soon, she'll be mine.*

CHAPTER 7

Ginny checked the screen for the hundredth time just to make sure she didn't miss anything important. It still showed the same progress bar, albeit it had changed from 5 percent to ... 6 percent.

Damn it.

With a resigned sigh, she pushed off from the desk and leaned back in the chair. She closed her eyes, breathing in the scent of soft, worn leather and the masculine scent she only knew as Gideon's distinct smell. Warmth pooled in her belly —and other bits of her—as she recalled the sight of his gorgeous, sexy torso and perfect six-pack abs.

Of course, she only had to turn and actually see it.

Don't do it. Don't do it. Don't do it.

Well, one short peek won't hurt, right?

Slowly, she swung the chair around, then let out a groan. Gideon lay flat on his back, arms splayed out, showing the defined muscles of his shoulders and the tattooed golden skin of his biceps and chest. The sheet rode low on his hips, drawing her attention to the perfect V of his Adonis belt.

What did I do in a past life that has the fates punishing me like this?

The man was temptation on a stick. Her lioness purred, licking its lips at the sight of the male flesh before them.

Hussy.

The animal snorted and flicked its tail.

"Ugh!" she exclaimed, then quickly shut her mouth as Gideon stirred. He let out a low moan, then turned on his side to show off the perfection of his back muscles.

Christ.

She swiveled the chair around to check on the progress of the program. *Still at six percent.* This was going to be a very long night.

Crossing her arms over the table, she rested her cheek on her forearms. Fatigue seeped into her muscles and bones. It had been ... more than three days now since she had any sleep. No wonder she felt like a gentle wind could knock her over. This was the point in her erratic sleep cycle that she eventually gave up because not even a shifter like her could go on without any rest for this long. Her eyes fluttered closed until darkness overtook her.

And once again the nightmares began.

Water. So much water. Around her, over her head. Into her lungs.

Kristos.

His face disappearing in the murky depths.

She struggled, legs kicking, arms flailing.

Ginny.

"Ginny!"

Her head shot up, but a vice-like grip tightened around her chest and she attempted to breathe. "No ..."

"Ginny ... Ginny ..." Strong arms slipped around her and under her knees, and she suddenly felt weightless. As Gideon's familiar, masculine scent surrounded her, she snapped out of her trance. His grip loosened, and oxygen slowly entered her lungs.

"It's all right. It's all going to be all right, *pusen*. It was just a dream."

He lay her down on something soft and pillowy. As her muscles relaxed, she felt a warm blanket cover her body.

"Sleep. I'm here. I won't let you go."

The words were like a balm, and try as she might, Ginny couldn't keep her eyes open. So, she shut them, but opened them moments later.

Huh.

An oddly refreshing feeling came over her as light hit her eyes.

Light?

She wasn't dreaming. The light filtering in through the sheer curtains was real. And so was the warm, muscled chest her cheek lay on.

Oh.

The steady rise and fall of Gideon's chest as well as the beat of his heart was definitely no dream. Her inner lioness purred at the feeling of their bodies pressed together, and desire pooled in her belly as she realized how close they were. Her head lay on his chest, arm slung over his waist. Though fully clothed in her server's outfit from the night before, the heat from his body warmed her. Lifting her gaze, she regarded his face, tracing the elegantly cut lines of his jaw, cheekbones, up to his thick blond lashes that any girl would kill for, before drifting down to those firm lips.

"I thought you said you didn't sleep," he whispered, the barest hint of a smile on his face. When she didn't answer, one eye cracked open, the golden amber orb fixed on her. "Good morning."

"Uh, good morning." When she attempted to move away, an arm snaked under her and pulled her on top of him. She let out a soft groan as the hard muscles of his torso and thighs pressed against hers, not to mention *other* hard parts of his body. A soft rumble emanated from his chest, and her own lioness answered with a satisfied purr.

Hands cupped her face, caressing her cheeks. Closing her eyes, she nuzzled against his calloused palm.

"What happened last night, Ginny? And yesterday at the beach."

She froze, her body seizing at the question. When she attempted to scramble off him, his arms wound around her, keeping her close.

"Let me—"

"Please, Ginny. I need to know what happened. And who is Kristos?"

"How did you ..."

"You said his name in your sleep. Is he ... important to you?"

Her throat burned, her instincts screamed at her to get out of there now and leave and never look at him again. But the soft, soothing rumbles from his chest calmed her. *Maybe if I tell him, he'd understand.* It might be the only way to push him away and keep him at arm's length. "Kristos ... he was my trainer and then partner when I joined The Agency."

"Was?"

She nodded. "Six months ago, we were on a mission. We

infiltrated a cell of an anti-shifter group that had ties to The Knights. They operated off an abandoned oil rig in international waters just off Malta. But things went south, and they had the place rigged with explosives. There was so much chaos and ... he and I fell into the water." Her lower lip trembled, and wetness streaked down her cheeks. "We got caught in some chains that dragged us down. I tried ... tried to break free and then suddenly the chains loosened. When I looked down, I realized he'd ... he'd freed me by slashing at the links with his claws." Like many of the residents of Lykos, Kristos had been a wolf shifter. "But he couldn't free himself, and I kept floating up higher and higher and—" A sob broke from her mouth.

"Oh gods. Ginny." His arms wrapped around her, holding her and cradling her tight. "Ginny, oh, Ginny." Hauling her up, he buried his nose in her hair. "It's all right. Let it out if you need to."

"I tried to dive back for him, but it was too late ... he's dead because of me." Guilt, anger, and deep sorrow drove a knife-like pain into her chest.

"No, *pusen*. Don't say that. Don't even think that."

"But it's true!"

"It was a tragedy, what happened to him. But as an agent, he probably knew the risks of his job. I think ... I think he made a choice. Allow both of you to drown or set you free so you could live."

"It's not fair."

"Oh, Ginny." He rolled her to her side, his hand reaching up to cup her face. "Don't say that."

"It's true. I should have died along—"

"*Don't.*"

The sheer agony in his tone made her heart stop. Her breath caught in her throat as she saw the expression of anguish on his handsome face.

They stared at each other until he spoke. "Was he ... were you ..."

"We weren't lovers if that's what you're asking. But we'd grown close." She didn't elaborate because Gideon wouldn't understand what it was like. She had spent nearly every waking moment training under Kristos for a year, then after that, they took on some pretty dangerous missions and had seen some horrific things. Their relationship seemed much more intimate than lovers.

"I'm so sorry for your loss." He reached out and pulled her closer, tucking her face into the crook of his neck. "Is that why you don't sleep?"

She nodded. "The nightmares ... they seem so real."

"I understand now. Why you acted that way at the beach yesterday. And I'm sorry if I dredged up bad memories for you."

"It's not your fault. You didn't know."

"Now I do. Thank you for telling me. For trusting in me."

She took in a whiff of his potent scent. A sudden strong urge made her want to take in more of him, so she nuzzled his neck, and his pulse jumped under her lips.

"Ginny," he groaned.

She just wanted to feel ... well, she just wanted to *feel*. To feel alive again and forget the numbness that had somehow been growing inside her these past months. *I shouldn't* ... But her body seemed to have a mind of its own as her mouth closed over the pulse point behind his ear.

He let out a deep growl, and before she knew it, he had

her on her back, his hips pinning her to the mattress, fingers entwining with hers to hold her hand down on either side of her head. Capturing her mouth, he kissed her savagely, all teeth and lips and tongue, and—God—it was exactly what she needed. She opened up to him, urging him to deepen the kiss. Knees nudged her thighs apart, and despite the layers of clothing between them, she could feel his substantial erection brushing up against her most intimate part.

She moaned into his mouth. He let go of her hands so he could attack the buttons on the front of her shirt, growing so impatient that he ripped the whole damn thing apart. *Holy shit!*

His large, warm hands cupped her breasts through her bra, fingers pulling down the cups so he could play with her already hardened nipples. She let out a mewl when his thumb and forefingers pinched at the nubs, the pressure just right to make her squirm as her panties flooded with her wetness.

His nostrils flared and those deep amber eyes darkened. Lowering his head, he took one nipple into his mouth, sucking hard, while a hand moved over her belly and tugged at the zipper of her pants. He eased them lower, and she helped him by lifting her hips. Tossing them aside, his fingers skimmed over the already-damp front of her panties. He teased her, rubbing her through the fabric, before yanking them to the side to plunge a finger into her slick pussy.

"Ungh!" She lifted her hips up, wanting more. He pressed another finger inside, caressing the most intimate parts of her. Releasing her nipple, he lowered himself, teasing the skin of her stomach and hips with his lips before he fully positioned his head between her thighs.

"I—oh!" The first touch of his mouth on her pussy sent zings of pleasure up and down her spine. He licked at her lips, caressing them with slow, purposeful motions. Her hips bucked up, but he grabbed them to hold her steady as he continued to taste her. When his tongue darted out at her clit, her eyes rolled to the back of her head.

She could have sworn she heard him hum with satisfaction, but the pleasure coursing through her system seemed to have temporarily blocked most of her senses. Only his touch, his mouth on her registered in her overstimulated brain as he slowly teased her to the edge of orgasm, holding back just enough before she could totally go over.

"Gideon," she moaned. "Let me ... I need ..."

His lips clamped around her clit and tongue flicking at her nub sent her over the edge, her body shuddering as the wave of pleasure washed over her, consuming her until she couldn't even think or move.

"Oh. God." Her fingers still clutched at the sheets, her mind reeling, her body slowly sinking back down into the mattress. Gideon continued to lick at her, cleaning up her juices. When she looked down, he met her gaze with a deep lust that she could feel right to her very bones. A gasp escaped her mouth when she saw that he had pushed his sweatpants down around his thighs and one hand gripped his enormous shaft, the bulbous head purple and dripping with pre-cum.

"Please, Ginny," he murmured against her skin as he kissed a path up her inner thighs, over her abdomen and between her breasts. "I need you so bad. Need to be in you."

"Yes," she moaned before he captured her mouth in a kiss. His hand splayed her thighs apart, hips positioning between them. She sucked in a breath, waiting for him to take her. The blunt end of his cock nudged at her entrance, and she spread her legs to accommodate him as he pushed forward.

"*Mother Frigga!*" he growled in annoyance.

"Yes! Wait, what?" Her eyes flew open. Above her, Gideon's face scrunched up in frustration as he withdrew from her. "Gideon?"

"I—Argh!" He threw a pillow over her naked body, then rolled off her. He flew toward the door, arms stretched out, though it opened before he could reach it.

"Bro!" Niklas called. "You're late for—"

"*Ack!*" Ginny clutched the pillow tighter to her chest, the heat of passion slowly leaving her body. "What the hell?"

Niklas's eyes went as large as saucers. "Oh. My. Gods."

"What part of 'don't come in here' didn't you understand?" Gideon grumbled.

"C'mon, bro," he tsked. "After thirty-three years, you still haven't learned that telling me *not* to do something is the best way to make sure I do something?"

"What are you doing in here?" Ginny cried.

"What am I doing here? I should be asking you that, shouldn't I?" He waggled his eyebrows at her.

"We were working," she huffed.

"Uh-huh." Niklas winked at her. "Right." He lifted his fingers to make air quotes. "Working."

Gideon grabbed his sweatpants and hopped into them. "Actually, we were—"

"The data!" Ginny took the sheet and pulled it over her body, then twisted it around her as she scampered off the bed.

Gideon's expression changed. "Right. It should be done now."

They both rushed toward his desk, nearly colliding into each other as they scrambled to check the progress of the data transfer. "Yes!" Ginny raised one fist in the air in triumph. "You did it!" She jumped up and kissed him square on the lips. "You're a genius, Gideon. A brilliant genius."

"Hmmm ..." His arms wound around her. "Tell me more."

"Well, you're also hot as—"

"Eww!" Niklas made a gagging sound and pretended to stick his finger down his throat. "Get a room, you two."

"We did, actually," Gideon pointed out. "Mine. What in Odin's name are you doing here, anyway?"

"Sorry to put a damper on your romantic interlude, but it's nine o'clock," he said matter-of-factly. "You were supposed to relieve me two hours ago."

"Oh Freya." Gideon released her and scrubbed his palm down his face. "I'm sorry. I, uh, overslept. Ginny and I were working on finding the mole."

Niklas snickered. "I'm sure you were."

"Niklas—"

"Gideon was helping me gather some data," Ginny explained. "And we might just have the evidence we need."

"What data?" Niklas asked. "And what kind of evidence?"

"From Minister Valens's phone." She briefed him about her suspicions and what had transpired during last night's dinner.

"Sounds like I missed out on some exciting times," Niklas

chuckled. "Man, I wish I could have been there to see Stein—"

Gideon cleared his throat. "Niklas, I'll report to duty now, but could you give us a minute?"

"Fine." He winked at them. "Don't take too long, okay? Though if you're anything like me—"

"Niklas!" Gideon warned.

"All right, All right." He put his hands up. "I'll be outside."

As soon as Niklas closed the door behind him, Gideon turned to her. "Sorry about ... Niklas."

"He's just being himself," she snorted.

"I should get ready for work," he grumbled, then headed to the bathroom.

Ginny sank down on the chair and turned to the screen. There was so much to do, and a lot of that data to comb through. But she couldn't think past that mind-blowing orgasm she'd experienced. And then after ... God, they'd nearly had sex. What was she thinking?

Her lioness mewled in annoyance, as if telling her, *stop thinking!*

She wanted him. There was no denying it. And he wanted her. Maybe she was going crazy. But then again, for the first time in months, she felt rested thanks to a nightmare-free sleep.

Sex with Gideon would complicate things right now, especially when she knew she would be leaving as soon as this case wrapped up. Rationality told her that she should stay away before either of them got hurt.

"Ginny?" Gideon called as he re-entered the bedroom.

His hair was damp from his shower, and he only wore a towel around his waist.

She groaned as she threw her dammed rationality out the window at the sight of his perfectly formed torso and boyish grin. He strode over to the dresser in the corner and pulled out some clothing. Without so much as a warning, he dropped the towel to the floor and began to dress, bending over to slip on his underwear and pants.

Holy Moly, I could bounce a quarter off that ass. "Are you leaving now?" she croaked, mouth dry as the Sahara.

Buttoning up his white linen shirt, he walked closer to her, hand reaching out to cup her face. "I really wish we hadn't been interrupted. Or that I didn't have to leave and attend to my duties."

"What time do you finish your shift?"

"I'll be with the king until lunch, then I'm on patrol until three. After that, I need to put some time doing some research at the library."

"Why don't I come see you then?" She covered his hand with hers and nuzzled at his palm.

An arm slipped around her waist and he pulled her close. "I'd like that." He pressed his lips to her temple, then trailed his mouth down her cheek before giving her a gentle kiss. "Make yourself comfortable and take all the time you need to review Valens's data. The program should already be starting with Ossler's phone."

"Thanks, I will."

"I'll see you later, Ginny," he said, his tone full of promise.

"See you."

As soon as he was gone, she sank back into the chair, her

knees barely able to keep her upright. *Fuck.* Planting her elbows on the desk, she buried her face in her hands.

"So ... things are going well with you and Gideon?"

She whipped her head toward the door where Niklas stood, a goofy grin on his face. "What goes on between me and Gideon is none of your business."

"Ugh, I don't want the gory details. I just—ew!" His face scrunched up.

"What's wrong now?"

"I just realized; you know what I look like naked now." He covered his chest with his hands. "I feel violated—hey!"

She chucked the first thing she could grab—the back pillow on the chair—at his head. "Don't you have somewhere to be?"

"I guess, but I do love watching you get all riled up, *systkin.*"

She rolled her eyes. "I have work to do." Swiveling the chair around, she grabbed the computer mouse and began to scroll through the contents of Valens's phone. Cracking her knuckles, she hunched over and began to sift through the data.

Ginny wasn't sure how much time had passed, but her eyes were dry and tired and her shoulders stiff by the time she pushed away from the desk. *But all the work had been worth it.*

"Did you find anything interesting?"

"Jeez—you're still here?" she exclaimed, rubbing her eyes

as she craned her neck up at Niklas. He stood over her, a tray in his hand.

"You were so absorbed in your work; I didn't want to disturb you." He lifted the tray. "Gideon wanted me to make sure you ate lunch."

"Lunch?" She glanced at the clock on the corner of the screen. "Jeez." She'd been working for hours.

He put the tray down next to her. "Eat. Or my brother will have my hide."

She sniffed, looking at the pile of sandwiches and the glass of orange juice on the tray. Her stomach grumbled, reminding her that she hadn't eaten or even drank anything for over twelve hours. She grabbed a sandwich and bit into it.

"So, did you find anything?"

Swallowing, she washed the turkey and cheese sandwich down with some juice. "Yeah. I think we might have some pretty damning evidence."

"Valens? Really?"

She nodded. "It took a while, but I cross-referenced his location data during the tour, along with his schedule. Though his work calendar only has him on official business, his phone data says otherwise. In Paris and Madrid, he took two side trips outside the city not listed in his schedule. And, check this out." She pulled up the map she created using the phone data. "See? On the day of the attack, he took a *vaporetto* to one of the smaller islands, but the security logs didn't mention that he'd left the hotel."

"So, he went on a little sightseeing tour by himself," Niklas said.

"Possible, but I went through all his text messages during

that time. He'd been texting this one particular number for a while now, even before the tour began. Check it out."

Tapping on the keyboard, she pulled up the messages she had found from the same number.

Valens: *European tour dates changed. Adjust plans accordingly. Will send along exact dates and places once confirmed.*
Unknown number: *Noted. Will wait for further advice.*

There were a few more exchanges regarding the cities on the tour itinerary and dates, and obviously ones where he met with his contact. However, it was the last exchange that Ginny found interesting.

Valens: *Need to see you NOW. Where can we meet in private?*
Unknown number: *Torcello. Church of Santa Maria Assunta. Four thirty.*

"I think Valens was meeting with whoever was responsible for the assassination attempt," Ginny said. "He was obviously hiding these meetings from the king. When he found out about the change in plan for dinner, he texted his contact so he could pass the info along."

Niklas wrinkled his nose. "That's possible, but what else do you have on him? Do any of the messages actually say anything about assassinating King Aleksei?"

"Unfortunately, no." She chewed at her lower lip. "But it's obvious he has something to hide."

"Treason is a serious crime, and unlike Karl, Valens is powerful and well-connected in the government. We can't just accuse him of conspiring with a foreign agent to assassinate the king without hard evidence."

She blew out a breath, sending a stray lock of hair flying. "If only I could find more solid evidence against him."

"A smart man like Valens wouldn't keep around anything that could link him to an assassin," Niklas began. "But he has to conduct his extracurricular activities somehow. At home, most likely."

"True. That means I need to break into his house and search it for any other evidence. I also have a device that can monitor and control any computer, but I'll need access to his PC to install it."

"It's not going to be easy."

"Why not?"

Niklas scratched at his chin. "A couple years ago, I accompanied Prince Harald to a private dinner at the Valens estate, just outside Odelia. Huge place. Like a fortress. And protected like one too."

"So? He has good security. Gideon can Cloak us and get me in, no prob."

"Yeah, you'd think that. But see, I chatted with some of his security people. First of all, he hires only the best, including this huge Kodiak bear shifter as his head of security. He has dogs and also other types of shifters patrolling the place twenty-four seven."

"Wow. Paranoid much?"

"Right? And he also has night vision and heat vision cameras covering the entire place."

"Hmmm." She thought for a moment. "Sounds like he doesn't want dragons who can turn invisible sneaking around his home." Which only made her even more suspicious of

Valens. The man definitely had something to hide, something he didn't want King Aleksei or his Dragon Guard to find out.

"Yeah, getting in there will be difficult."

"Unless we were invited in." She shot to her feet. "I'm going to go see the queen. I bet she could invite herself to his house. Maybe for a social visit, along with the prince and his nanny. Does Valens have a wife? Or kids?"

Niklas shrugged. "I'm not sure."

"All right, I'll ask the queen. Thanks, Niklas."

"Anytime, *systkin*."

She left Niklas and snuck back to her room so she could change out of last night's uniform and into a fresh pair of leggings and a ruffled blouse. Then, she headed to the queen's office, however, the receptionist told her Sybil went back to the royal apartments. So, she headed straight there and breezed right in.

"Oh good, you're here, Your Majesty." Sybil sat by herself on the plush couch in the living area. "I have some important news." Flouncing over to her, she plopped down next to the queen.

Sybil pursed her lips together. "Uh, Gin—"

"We were able to extract the data from Valens's phone. You won't believe what I found out. I hope you're not too shocked, but I think he could be the one responsible for the assassination attempt."

"Ginny!" Sybil's silvery eyes grew wide.

She let out an exasperated sigh. "What?" Then she noticed the queen's rigid posture and her gaze, which was fixed somewhere behind Ginny, just above her shoulder. Her stomach flipped at the realization they were not alone. Slowly, she turned her head. "Oh fuck."

Standing in the threshold that led in from the nursery was Poppy, along with Lady Vera, who held Prince Alric in her arms.

"Uh, have they been there the entire time?" she whispered to Sybil.

The queen slapped a hand to her forehead. "That's what I was trying to tell you."

Lady Vera sauntered over to them and handed Prince Alric to the queen, who eagerly reached out for his mother. "He was in a good mood when we came in to wake him up from his nap." Then she turned her pretty violet eyes at Ginny. "I knew there was something not quite right with you."

"How?" Ginny asked.

"You mispronounced the diphthongs in Nordgensprak the same way Her Majesty does." She gave Sybil an apologetic smile. "So, you are American. What are you doing here? Obviously, you're not a server and you're familiar with our queen. Did you know her back in Colorado?"

"It's all right, I trust Lady Vera with my life," Queen Sybil said as she wrangled Prince Alric in her lap. "Lady Vera, this is Ginny Russel. She's here to investigate the assassination attempt." And so, the queen gave a quick rundown of what had happened so far.

Lady Vera placed a hand on her chest. "Oh my. I'm very grateful you're here to catch the blackguards trying to hurt the royal family."

"I almost forgot why I came here." Ginny explained what she had found out about Valens and why she needed access to his house.

"Hmmm, it shouldn't be a problem to invite myself to his

home. I am the queen," Sybil said. "But we just had him over for dinner last night, and he might find it suspicious considering his contentious history with the royal family. And I'm not sure how I can justify bringing Alric and Ginny along."

"Does the minister have a wife or children you can pay a social call to?" Poppy asked.

"I'm afraid not. Unfortunately, Minister Valens's wife passed away last summer, and he has no children."

Ginny felt a twinge of sadness for the man, but she had to remember Valens could be guilty of treason. "We'll have to think of another reason to have me there."

Lady Vera raised a hand. "I have an idea."

"You do?" Ginny asked.

"Yes. Um ..." She bit her lip. "Last night, Minister Valens expressed his, uh, interest in seeing me socially."

"Socially?" Ginny snapped her fingers when it dawned on her. "Oh, he wants to date you?"

"I suppose you can say that."

"But he's, like, so old." Ginny slapped her hand over her mouth when Lady Vera grimaced. "Uh, sorry."

"There's something to be said about a mature man," Poppy interjected diplomatically. "Like, er, fine wine, an older man would be more refined and settled. He's sown his wild oats, as they say."

Ginny cleared her throat. "If you don't mind me saying, Lady Vera, you're a babe. You should find yourself a hot young guy who makes your eyes roll to the back of your head. There's so many of them around here."

Lady Vera's cheeks turned red. "Minister Valens is not *so* old that he wouldn't be able to give me children. And my father would certainly approve of the match." She shuddered. "But if he's part of the plot to assassinate the king, then I would never consider him. But, as I said, perhaps I could use his interest to our advantage."

Ginny leaned forward, curious. "Oh? How?"

"I'll accept his invitation to dinner, but insist it be a private affair to protect my reputation. After all, his wife hasn't even been gone a year."

"How are you going to get Ginny inside his house?" Queen Sybil asked.

"You could disguise yourself once again and say you are my maid," Lady Vera suggested. "And that my father insisted I bring you along. Then I can distract him, while you snoop around his home."

"That's brilliant!" Ginny exclaimed.

"You don't have to do that, Lady Vera," Sybil said, patting her hand. "It's not fair to drag you into this. And who knows what Valens might do if he finds out you were involved."

"It would be an honor, my queen," Lady Vera replied. "I may not be a trained agent like Ginny or a member of the Dragon Guard, but I want to do my part in stopping any threat to the kingdom or our royal family."

"I won't get caught," Ginny promised. "Besides, if we don't find any evidence, then at least we can take him off the suspect list. No harm, no foul."

"See? Everything will work out, Your Majesty," Lady Vera assured her.

"All right," the queen agreed. "But we're going to have to let Aleksei and Rorik in on this plan."

And Gideon, she thought silently. But something told her he wasn't just going to let her walk into Valens's house so easily, not if the last two times she tried to investigate her suspects were any indication. He'd probably try to horn in on her mission and find a way to insinuate himself into her plan. While he'd been helpful the last two times, he might actually be a liability this time because Valens knew him. If they got caught, Valens would know the king suspected him of treason, and who knew what he'd do? At least if she went in alone, she could pretend she was stealing valuables and Lady Vera would have plausible deniability. Hopefully, Gideon would listen to reason.

CHAPTER 8

"I'm glad you're safely back in the Assyrian Mountains, Thoralf." Gideon adjusted the screen of his laptop and expanded the video chat window as he spoke with his former captain.

"Thank you," Thoralf replied. "The late winter storms had made the journey difficult. But I am finally here. In the morning, I shall once again meet with the tribal elders so they can tell me more about the wand."

In his previous research, Gideon had found a photo of a similar wand from the archives of the Oxford Department of Anthropology. This particular wand had been in the possession of a tribe in the Assyrian Mountains. Unfortunately, it had been stolen from them which was why Thoralf had abandoned that lead. But now that they had confirmed this was the same one used in the Venice attack, Thoralf decided to go back and speak with the tribal elders to gather more information.

"Ask them if they have any records of when they

acquired the wand and how they used it, as well as if it has shown any other magical properties," Gideon suggested.

"Excellent. If that is all, I shall rest for now so I may be refreshed by morning."

"All right." Gideon paused. "And, Thoralf?"

"Yes?"

"I know I haven't mentioned it before but ... I want to apologize."

"Apologize?" Thoralf's golden brows drew together. "For what?"

He sighed. "For sending you on these wild goose chases. It's been over two years since you've gone on your quest, and we still haven't found a cure for Prince Harald. And—"

"My friend." Thoralf raised a hand. "Do not be so hard on yourself. And you are not to blame for Prince Harald's current condition."

Gideon knew the former captain blamed himself, of course, for failing to protect the prince. "And neither are you. The Knights attacked us, and if you were the one who had your dragon taken away, I'm sure King Aleksei would not stop until we found the cure either." Thoralf, after all, was practically a brother to Aleksei and son to Prince Harald.

"Thank you, my friend." There was a sad smile on his face. "Do not fret. We will restore our king's dragon. But I must say, seeing the world has been an exhilarating experience."

"You've probably circled the globe several times now," Gideon said.

"Yes. I have seen a great many wonders. Though ... I do long for home." He looked Gideon straight on. "I have every confidence that you will find the clue to lead us to the cure."

"Well, hopefully I'll have time to do more research. Has the king filled you in on the other projects we are working on?"

"Ah, yes. The mole and the lost prince. How goes that search?"

"It's ... going." He updated Thoralf on what he had found out about the missing Dragon Guard.

"A conundrum indeed," Thoralf commented. "But I have every faith you will solve this mystery, as well as that of who attempted to assassinate our king." The corner of his mouth quirked up. "Speaking of which, I hear congratulations are in order. In honor of your finding your mate."

Gideon groaned. "Niklas told you, too?"

Thoralf's laughter boomed through the speakers. "He was quite delighted that you have found the other half of your soul. And from Blackstone to boot, like our queen. Tell me, have you forged the bond with her yet?"

"I'm ... working on it."

"Of course, you both have much responsibilities. But I have every faith you shall win the lady lioness's heart."

"Thank you, Thoralf." They said their goodbyes, then Gideon hung up. Closing his laptop lid, he let out a breath. Everyone seemed positive that his and Ginny's mating was a done deal. *If only I had their confidence.* Sure, this morning had been a step in the right direction, and he was so certain now that Ginny would be the only woman for him. Had they not been interrupted ...

He groaned, feeling his cock stir at the memory. How she tasted, the smell of her as she came on his mouth. Her sweet, soft body yielding to him, how tight and hot—

He scrubbed a hand down his face. Technically, he was

still on duty, and he had work to do. Besides, later tonight, once they were alone, he and Ginny could finish what they started, hopefully uninterrupted.

After a few deep breaths to calm his raging hormones, he grabbed his laptop, left his apartment, and proceeded to the library. Now that Thoralf was able to make his way back to the Assyrian tribe, Gideon could work on his research on the Grand Duke Aleksandr and the missing Dragon Guard.

According to King Aleksei's great aunt, Princess Natalia, one of the private investigators she hired found a witness that said they had spotted a dragon flying near a lake where Zaratena used to be, right by the border between Belarus and Ukraine. He pulled up the interview transcript from the witness and began to read for what seemed like the hundredth time, trying to scour for any morsel of information that might lead to the whereabouts of the dragon. While the interview had been done in Ukranian, the English translation was printed below the original.

Interviewer: *Describe the events of the day you spotted this creature.*
Pyotr Ivicic: *I was hunting for mushrooms in the forest when I heard a loud flapping sound. I looked up, and between the high tree branches, I saw the creature. Fast wings. Body like a reptile. Its scales were so bright, I was blinded for a moment.*
Interviewer: *Which direction was it headed?*
Pyotr Ivicic: *Toward the lake. I followed it, ran as fast as I could. I saw another flash of pure light, then it was gone.*

He scrubbed a hand down his face. There was nothing there that could indicate the creature he saw was indeed a

Dragon Guard. Or the Dragon Guard. *If he even existed,* he mused. *Why would we not have any record of him? Not even a mention of his House?*

He went back to the shelf where the volumes of the *History of the Dragon Families of the Northern Isles* were located. Picking up *Volume* 12, he leafed through the table of contents for an overview.

"Anyone ever tell you how adorable you look when you're concentrating?"

Gideon's dragon perked up at the sound of their mate's voice. He lifted his head, and sure enough—there she was, leaning against the shelf, arms casually crossed over her chest, and a saucy grin on her lovely face.

"I thought I'd find you here."

"I didn't think you'd come by so soon."

She sauntered over to him. "Should I come later then?"

"No!" He snapped the book shut and laid it on the shelf. "I mean ... this is a pleasant surprise."

Reaching out, she cupped the side of his face. "That frown says otherwise."

"It's not you, *pusen*." He closed his eyes and leaned into her touch. "Just ... work."

"Tell me what's wrong."

Gideon had never been the type to unload his feelings on anyone. Indeed, with his reserved and private nature, he preferred to keep his emotions to himself. However, Ginny's soothing touch and presence somehow broke a dam in him. "Some days, I just feel like a failure. This is my duty, and I want to serve my king and country, but when nothing I do makes a difference, I can't help but feel helpless." He told her about all the research he'd been doing, not only in finding a cure for The Wand, but also in finding the lost prince.

"I had no idea." She stepped into his arms and embraced him. "And it's not fair they pile this on you."

He kissed her temple. "It is my duty."

"But they're expecting way too much of you." He felt her frown against his chest, then she lifted her head. "Or are you expecting too much of yourself?"

He grimaced.

"I thought so." She smirked. "Gideon, you're only one man. A brilliant man, yes, but you can't possibly think you can handle all of that work on your own." Stepping away from him, she grabbed his arm. "Turn around."

"I beg your pardon?"

"I said, turn around."

Shrugging, he followed her instructions. "What—oh." Her fingers dug into his shoulders, thumbs zeroing in on the knots he never even knew were there. "I ... oh ... that's good." His body loosened under her ministrations, and he braced himself against the shelves. "Where did you learn to do that?"

Her hands moved lower, finding all the achy parts of his back and kneading away the tenseness he hadn't even real- ized was there. "I took a Thai massage course in Bangkok."

"Oh." He groaned embarrassingly loud when she hit a certain spot at the bottom of his spine. "Ginny. That's—" He sucked in a breath when she leaned forward, hands moving to his front, her fingers teasing his abdomen. "Is this part of the massage?"

She hummed noncommittally as she pressed her body along his back. He could feel her soft breasts against him as her hands moved lower.

"Gin ..." His teeth dug into his lip when she dipped into the waistband of his trousers. She wrapped her fingers around his cock, instantly stroking it to full hardness. His brain told him this wasn't the place for this, that they could get caught ... but somehow, that only aroused him more.

The pleasure spread across his body like a wave as Ginny continued to stroke him, her fingers gripping him tight. He was so close.

As if sensing his impending orgasm, she slowed her movements, and he let out a relieved sigh, not wanting to come too soon. But before he could gather his thoughts, she spun him around, then pushed him until his back hit the shelves.

She smiled like the Cheshire Cat as she knelt down in front of him and made quick work of the fastening on his trousers and pulled them down, along with his underwear. His cock bobbed painfully and her hands encircled him, her tongue flicking out to lick at her plush lips as she moved her head forward.

"Ginny!" The back of his head hit the solid wood shelves with a loud thud as her lips wrapped around the bulbous head of his cock. She let out a moan as she slid down, taking more of him into her wet, hot mouth.

"*Odin's beard!*" Unsure where to put his hands, he held onto the wooded shelving for dear life. The boards creaked under his grip, and he would have broken them into pieces had he not stopped himself. Ginny's mouth and lips continued to pleasure him, her head bobbing up and down enthusiastically. Dear gods, he was nearly there. But he gathered every ounce of his self-control and dug his fingers into her hair to slow her down, then pull her away. Before she could protest, he hauled her up, switched their positions, then gave her a savage kiss. She responded just as fiercely, her hands clawing at his shoulders.

"Yes?" he asked against her mouth.

"Oh, yes."

He didn't need further invitation as he stuck his thumbs into the waistband of her leggings and panties, then yanked them to her ankles. He pulled her up and planted her ass on one of the lower shelves. Pushing his own trousers and under-wear down, he spread her thighs and slid a finger along her naked slit. She was already slick and ready. Part of him wished they were in his bed or any bed, so he could take his time with her.

"Now, Gideon," she groaned, her hips bucking against his hand. "Please."

This was right, he told himself as he placed the tip of his cock against her wet, waiting entrance. Gritting his teeth, he buried his face in her neck and pushed forward, inch by inch so she could accommodate him until he was all the way inside.

"Are you okay?" His lips brushed against her soft skin.

"One ... sec."

He breathed in her intoxicating scent. Gods, her grip around him was tight, and his brain was so overstimulated that he feared he would spill himself before giving her any pleasure. Lifting his head, he looked down at her beautiful face, then leaned down to kiss her sweet lips again, softly this time, savoring the feel and taste of her. Like sunshine or a fresh spring rain. Or maybe it was just ... Ginny.

Slowly, her hips moved against him, and as if she wasn't already gripping him tight, she squeezed harder, making him groan. Steadying her with his hands, he pulled back until only the tip of his cock remained inside her, then thrust in quickly.

She yelped, and her fingers dug into his shoulders. Knees tightened around his hips as he continued to move in and out of her.

She met him thrust for thrust, her hips slamming against him as if he wasn't already riding her hard. Her body shuddered, and she pressed her mouth against his shoulder to muffle her cries. He continued his pace and focused on the feel of being inside her and in his arms as she came apart. His eyes rolled to the back of his head at the way her inner muscles squeezed him, but by some miracle of the gods, he didn't come. Oh no, he wasn't finished with her, not by a long shot.

He withdrew from her, making her whimper. "Shh ... *pusen*. I'm not done yet."

"Gideon—oh!"

In one motion, he flipped her around, pressing her up against the shelves. Grabbing her wrists, he placed them above her head, pinning them with one hand. His other hand slid down her body, kneading her breasts through her clothes before moving lower between her legs. He found her clit, already engorged and sensitive, her scent exploding in his nose as he pinched it.

"Gah!" Her body shook again, and before she could come down from her orgasm, he grabbed his shaft and slid all the way into her.

"So hot and tight," he murmured in her ear. "I've been dreaming about your pussy since I met you, my little lioness."

"Gideon," she moaned in a needy voice as she pushed her hips back. "Fuck me, please."

"Don't you worry." He pulled back, then thrust in quickly, making her yelp. "Later, when we go to my room, you can scream your head off." And he planned to keep her screaming all night. "For now, you'll have to be quiet. Can you do that for me?"

She nodded, biting her lip. "Yes."

"Good girl." He nudged her hair away from her neck, then gave her nape a hard nip. Instantly, she flooded around him. "Ginny ..."

He reached for her clit again. When he found it, he plucked at the nub as he fucked into her. He surged in and out, the drag of her tight passage sending zings of pleasure down his spine. The tingling there began, signaling that he was right at the edge. When he gave her clit one more pinch, she let out a muffled cry, so he hammered into her even harder. She squeezed around him, and he slammed in one last time as he felt his release take over. He exploded inside her, the pleasure short-circuiting his brain. He could see and feel the pulse in her neck thrum wildly, so he sank his teeth into it, making her convulse and milk every drop of cum from him.

For a moment, he stopped breathing. Thinking. His heart seemed to cease beating as well as his body function was reduced to that one moment of pure bliss.

As he came back to his senses, he finally realized why the French call it *la petite mort*. The little death indeed.

"Oh God," she panted. "Did we really just—"

"Yes," he croaked.

"Right here in the—"

"Yes." Pulling out of her, he whirled her around and planted his mouth on hers in a slow, sensuous kiss. She melted into him, returning his kisses with a fervent ardor. When they finally pulled away, they were breathless once again.

"Well, that's one way to take that frown off your face."

He laughed aloud, throwing his head back. "I guess it is."

They began to re-dress and right themselves, though it took a while because she kept distracting him with small kisses and touches here and there.

"So," she said, picking up the book he had placed on the shelf. "Exciting reading?"

"I wish. It's about the history of the dragon families in The Northern Isles."

"Dragon families?"

"Yes. We have ten in total now, but in the beginning, there were more families on the isles. And more dragons as well."

"How long have dragons lived here?"

"Our recorded history goes back to 793. However, our oral traditions indicate the first dragons settled here at least five hundred years before that."

"Wow." Turning the book on its side, she scrunched her eyes at the spine. "That book has the entire history of all the dragon families?"

"I'm afraid this is only the twelfth volume of fifteen," he said wryly. "I've been making my way back."

"Huh." She thought for a moment. "With such a long history ... could it be possible your missing Dragon Guard could have come from a family that doesn't exist anymore?"

He blinked. "I suppose. He could have been orphaned." It made sense. There were less and less dragons every generation, with so few females being born. In fact, there hadn't been a female of their kind born in The Northern Isles in over fifty years.

"So, what happens to orphaned dragon children?"

"Usually, they're fostered with another family or sent to an orphanage. Our former captain, Thoralf, for example, was a ward of Prince Harald. He had no other living relatives and thus the last of his house."

"So, it's possible that the missing Dragon Guard had been orphaned with no living relatives? And that's why none of the other families have any record of him?"

"Mother Frigga, you could be on to something!" He grabbed her shoulders and kissed her square on the mouth. "You're amazing." His inner animal snorted in agreement.

A smile curled up her lips. "Hey, maybe all you needed was that massage to relax you and clear your head."

He pushed her back against the same shelf where he had taken her minutes ago. "Since you're here then, maybe you can help me relax some more? Clear more of my—"

"Gideon? Where—oh."

They turned to where the voice came from. Sure enough, Wesley Baxter stood at the end of the aisle, mouth hanging open.

Gideon released Ginny. "Hey, uh, Wes. How are you? I mean ..." He cleared his throat and strode toward him. Kneeling down to his level, he spoke in a soft tone. "I'm glad you're here."

His head cocked to the side. "You are?"

"Yes. I was harsh with you and I apologize. I had a terrible day, but that's no excuse. And you were right to come to me for help. I promise you, if you need anything, anything at all, I will always aid you anyway I can."

"Oh." He paused, as if contemplating something. Then, he leaned close to his ear. "Niklas told me everything. About you and Ginny being mates."

"Of course he did," he muttered.

"And he said that you and your dragon were fighting because you were confused, which was why you acted so mean to me. But that once you and Ginny were in the mates zone, you'd be all better." He looked back at Ginny and then to him. "Well, are you in the mates zone?" He sniffed at him. "You smell like her. Similar to the way Mum smells like Rorik when he stays over."

"I, uh ..." Gideon scratched at the back of his head. "We're headed there. To the mates zone."

"Good." Wesley patted him on the shoulder. "I like her. My cheetah likes her and her lioness too."

He grinned. "I like her a lot too."

"Everything okay?" Ginny approached them tentatively.

"Yes," he said. "I just realized I hadn't apologized to Wesley for my rudeness the other day."

"And I accepted," Wesley added.

A warm smile lit up her face. "That's great, Wesley."

"I'm going to do my assignments here, if that's okay, Gideon? Then I'll head back in an hour when Mum comes home."

"Of course, stay as long as you like. I have some homework to do too."

"Actually, maybe I can help Gideon with his homework too." She winked at him.

"You already did, *pusen*," he replied and waggled his eyebrows at her in a very Niklas-like way.

Her brows furrowed together. "You keep calling me that ... *pusen*. What does it mean?"

"It means 'my kitten.'" That's what she was. His. And at this point, she pretty much owned him too.

A blush crept up her cheeks. "And Niklas ... he called me *systkin*."

He couldn't stop the corners of his mouth from turning up even if he tried. *Sister*, Niklas had called her. "You should ask him." Leaning over, he said in a low voice. "How about when Wesley leaves, we go back to my room." More specifically, his bed.

Her body stiffened. "Oh. Um, actually, I'll have to take a rain check on that."

"Rain check?"

"Yeah. I sort of, have to, uh, go with Lady Vera, sneak into Minister Valens's house, and find evidence that he's the mole," she babbled. "So, yeah, I'll see you later, okay?" And with that, she was gone in a flash.

It took Gideon a few seconds to process her words.

"What?"

CHAPTER 9

Ginny hightailed it out of the library but wasn't really banking on outrunning Gideon. However, she thought she'd make it farther than the threshold before he caught up to her, grabbed her, and spun her around.

"What do you mean you're sneaking into Minister Valens's house?" he roared, trapping her in his arms. "Do you know how dangerous that is? His estate is more secure than Fort Knox! What if you were discovered?"

"I won't get—"

"I changed my mind." They froze as Wesley calmly walked out of the library, his schoolbag slung over his shoulder. "I'm going back home now."

"Great idea, Wes," Ginny said. "Let me walk you back." She attempted to wiggle out of Gideon's embrace, but his grip remained strong.

"Have a good night, Wesley." Gideon's gaze didn't stray from her. "Well?" he asked when the boy was out of earshot.

"Funny thing." She let out a fake laugh. "All that data

your handy little device got from Valens's phone? Weeeeellll, I found a lot of valuable information on it. But not enough." Briefly, she told him about what she had discovered on the minister's mobile.

"So, you conjured up this crazy plan to sneak into Valens's house? And you weren't planning on telling me, were you?"

"Only because I knew you'd overreact or try to stop me. Which you're doing right now, by the way."

He gritted his teeth. "Is that why you had sex with me? To lull me into—"

"What?" Anger bubbled in her chest. "How dare you!" Using her full strength, she escaped his grip and pushed him away. "How could you say that? Do you think I'm the kind of person who would use sex to get what I want?"

His expression faltered. "Ginny, no! Of course not. I'm sorry." He raked his fingers through his hair and approached her with slow and tentative steps. "Please ... don't think that. I know you would never ... what happened here ... it was amazing."

The sincerity in his voice plucked at her heart. And the memories slammed right into her brain, making her all warm and tingly. Her lioness purred in delight, rolling on its back and showing its belly. "I wanted it. Wanted you. For real." It was all real. So real that she could barely keep the wave of terror threatening to overwhelm her at bay.

"I know, *pusen*." His shoulders relaxed. "All right, tell me your plan."

This was the last thing she wanted. She shouldn't have gone to him. Should have just left with Lady Vera so she could finish the case and move on. She didn't want his help or have him around.

"Ginny?"

His hand caressed her arm gently, sending a tingle up her skin. "Lady Vera is having dinner at Minister Valens's house. We're going to pretend I'm her maid, then while she honey traps him, I'm going to plant a remote access device on his computer."

"Honey trap? She's going to sleep with him?"

"Ew, no, not *that* kind of honey trap. Just keep him busy, but she won't take it that far." At least, she hoped not. Lady Vera seemed eager to help with their plan, maybe even excited at the prospect, but the thought of her sleeping with the slimy man caused her stomach to turn.

"And the king and queen agreed to this?"

"Well, the queen did. She should be telling him now."

"All right, let's go see them."

As they made their way to the royal apartments, Ginny prepared herself for all kinds of scenarios when they met with King Aleksei. She expected the king might not easily agree to the plan, but surely, he'd listen to reason.

When they entered the suite, however, what she didn't expect was the statue—er, Stein—raising his voice to Their Majesties as he stretched out to full height, hulking shoulders hunched forward.

"You cannot allow this, Your Majesty!" he growled loudly in a rough, grating tone. "This is dangerous."

The king nodded. "I agree with you, Stein. If they are caught—"

"But we're not going to be caught!" Ginny objected as she marched toward them, hands on her hips.

King Aleksei pinned her with his ocean-colored gaze. "Is that so?"

She gulped as she sensed the king's dominant dragon. Bowing her head, she spoke in a calm voice. "Yes. I mean, obviously I can't guarantee that, but I'm a professional, Your Majesty. I've gone through more dangerous missions than this. I've dealt with kidnappers, drug dealers, sex traffickers, anti-shifter terrorists. I can handle one politician."

"Minister Valens is not someone you want to make an enemy of," Gideon said. "We should find another way."

"There is no other way. Your Majesty?" she pleaded to Sybil.

All eyes turned to the queen. "This plan has its dangers," Sybil began. "But any and all the things we've been doing to find this mole have been risky. What if Karl had been the mole and saw you following him? He could have been armed. Or what if Luster had been working with The Knights and had some kind of magical weapon? Or if Ossler, Valens, or Melina caught you trying to steal their phones, and they felt trapped and lashed out in some way? The truth is, finding this traitor is our top priority." Her lower lip trembled. "Aleksei, seeing you hurt nearly killed me. I want them found *now*, before they even have a chance to come after you or Alric again."

Hope soared in Ginny, though it was dampened by the expression of defeat on Gideon's face. *No, don't think that. This was why she was here. Remember the mission.*

The king let out a breath. "You must take every precaution."

"Your Majesty!" Stein protested. "You can't—" But the stern look from his king silenced him.

"Thank you, Your Majesty." She breathed a sigh of relief. "And I'll make sure this doesn't blow back on you."

"I'll come with you," Gideon interjected.

"No, I will," Stein said.

"No, *I* will," Gideon insisted.

"Why you?"

"You *know* why."

She planted her hands on her hips. "And where are you two going to hide? Under Lady Vera's skirt? There's not even room for one of you there."

Gideon ground his teeth together. "I can hide in the trunk of the limousine."

"*I* will go in the limo," Stein shot back.

Stupid bull-headed men! "Oh my God, stop it you two, no one is coming with me."

The queen rubbed her temple with her fingers. "Oh dear."

"You're not going to fit in that boot, Stein." Gideon countered. "It'll be a tight fit for me, but they wouldn't even be able to close the lid with you in there."

"He's got a point there, Stein," the king agreed. "But I would feel better if one of you were there."

"Worst-case scenario, I'll pretend I'm stealing cash and jewelry if Valens catches me," Ginny reasoned. "That would limit the investigation into Valens, but it's not the end of the world." *But I don't plan on getting caught*, she added silently. She was determined to find the evidence they needed to pin the assassination attempt on Valens or totally clear him so she could move on.

"This is a crazy idea." King Aleksei shook his head. "But I suppose sending the ministry police to arrest Valens on what

weak evidence we currently have would create greater polit-
ical consequences."

"Gideon will go with you," Sybil said. "Only to keep us
up to date with what's happening and let us know when
you've succeeded and are safely out of the minister's home."

"But also to warn us just in case something goes wrong, so
we can prepare accordingly," the king added. "Gideon, you
must not be seen at his estate."

No one said it aloud, but Ginny knew what it meant. If
Valens saw any Dragon Guard breaking into his home, he'd
know King Aleksei was involved, and it would destroy His
Majesty politically.

Stein opened his mouth, but clamped it shut before
storming out of the room.

"Wow, what bug got up his ass?" Ginny muttered. "Fine,
Gideon can come, but *only* as an observer."

"It's settled then," King Aleksei declared. "Come back
here as soon as you can. We will be waiting the entire
evening until you all are safely back."

"We will, Your Majesty." With a deep bow, Gideon
ushered them outside.

"That was sneaky of you," she said, miffed.

He turned to her, his expression growing dark. "You
think I would have let you walk in there by yourself, alone
and unprotected?"

The possessive gleam in his eyes shot a bolt of desire
down to her core that both excited and infuriated her. "I told
you, I've been doing this a while now. This is just a routine
mission, what I signed up for. You should understand that
most of all."

"I do, *pusen*." His tone softened, and he touched her

cheek with his palm. "Why can we not work together then, with this common goal? Besides, my queen said I must go with you, and I must obey my queen."

Her heart thudded in her chest. She knew why. And it wasn't because of what had transpired between them. Casual sex, she could handle. It was everything else that came with it, with him, that had her running in the other direction. Letting him get too close and under her skin had been her mistake.

No, she couldn't stay here.

Just finish this job.

Then what?

Leave this place. Move on. Keep moving, outrun the nightmares and the guilt.

Her lioness did not like that, but she shut it away before it could object.

"Ginny?"

"Yes?" She swallowed to moisten her dry throat. "I mean, yes, we should get to work."

CHAPTER 10

Lady Vera had been eager to help with their plan from the beginning, and she even offered to prepare Ginny before they went to Minister Valens's house. So, she and Gideon proceeded to the Solveigson estate once Lady Vera confirmed the dinner plans.

"What do you think?" Ginny asked as she stepped out of the massive walk-in closet–vanity area.

"I hardly recognize you," Lady Vera said, astonished.

Ginny had put on extra makeup to darken her brows and get rid of her freckles, plus a plain, mousy brown wig that she left braided and tucked under a white cap that matched her drab gray maid's uniform. "Yeah, a little makeup and different hair can make all the difference." She stepped back, dropped her hands to her side, slumped her shoulders forward and cast her gaze down, as she had observed the other maids in the palace did whenever the queen walked by.

"Simply amazing," Lady Vera remarked. "Is acting part of your training?"

"Yeah. Disguises aren't worth anything if you can't sell it."

"Initially, I was worried that Minister Valens might recognize you from the dinner, but I think that won't be a problem now."

"As long as I keep my mouth shut, I should be fine." She also practiced a few lines of Nordgensprak with Lady Vera for the 'performance' later on. "Besides, from what I observed, Minister Valens isn't the type to notice servants."

Indeed, that night as she served him dinner, the man didn't even look her in the eye much less the face, as if she were some lower form of life. That was evident, too, in his actions, from the way he snapped his fingers at the servers to catch their attention when he wanted his wine glass refilled and sneered at them when he thought they were too slow. *Ugh.* While Ginny herself had grown up privileged, her mother would have torn her a new one if she ever treated their housekeeper or other staff that way.

Lady Vera checked her watch. "We should get going, we don't want to be late."

Ginny remained in character, keeping her head down as they headed out of Lady Vera's room, down to the main house, then out toward the spacious foyer where a butler opened the door for them.

"Thank you, Maxwell. Has the car been brought around?"

"Yes, my lady."

They walked out to the driveway where the limo was parked, waiting for them. Ginny couldn't help the way her heart drummed in her chest as she glanced at the vehicle's trunk.

Lady Vera cleared her throat and turned to face her. "Greta, did you remember to bring my red make-up bag?" she asked in Nordgensprak.

"*Ja, min damme,*" Ginny replied. *C'mon, Gideon.*

Before they arrived at the Solveigson estate, she and Gideon came up with a plan for him to sneak into the limo. He would Cloak himself and wait in the garage, then slip into the trunk. The exchange about the red makeup bag was his cue to let her know that he had succeeded.

Focusing her enhanced hearing, she waited for the reply.

Rap. Rap. Rap.

The breath she didn't even realized she'd been holding escaped her lungs. *He made it!* Gideon should be sending a message to the king and queen via his phone to inform them that the next phase of their plan was about to begin. She nodded at Lady Vera to let her know they were good to go.

The other woman returned it with a nod of her own, then turned expectantly toward the limo. They stood there for a few seconds, neither of them moving.

Ginny glanced around. "Is everything okay?" she asked in a soft tone.

Lady Vera's brows furrowed, her pretty violet eyes narrowed. "Must be a new driver," she muttered. "Oh well." She squared her shoulders and opened the limo door herself before slipping inside. Ginny followed and settled in beside Lady Vera on the buttery soft leather seats.

Lady Vera said a few words to the driver up front, who only grunted a curt affirmative without looking back before the automatic shades lifted in place.

"Why, I never!" she harrumphed.

"Can't get good help these days, huh?" Ginny joked.

"Apparently."

As Lady Vera smoothed her perfectly manicured hands down the front of her dress, Ginny noticed the slight tremor in her fingers. "It's okay to be nervous," Ginny began. "You'll be fine. First mission's always the hardest.

Lady Vera managed a tense chuckle. "I don't know how you do it. In fact, I can't believe you do this all the time. If it were me, I'd fall apart immediately."

"You're very brave to be doing this."

"I wish I could do more to help. Not just with finding this traitor but also with all the other problems King Aleksei and Queen Sybil are facing." She let out a sigh. "I feel so useless sometimes. Like I wish I'd done more to better myself while growing up instead of spending my days shopping or going to parties."

"It's not too late yet, believe me," Ginny said with a chuckle. "Um, so I know I said I'd been doing this a while now, but the truth is ... I've only been with The Agency a little over two years and a year of that was just training." She gave Lady Vera a rundown of how she had lived a nomadic life before joining The Shifter Protection Agency.

"Your life sounds so exciting. And now you're actually making a difference in people's lives." She tsked. "Some people could be so cruel."

A chill ran over her. *You don't even know the half of it.* The things she'd seen hadn't even been the worst of it, at least, that's what Kristos had told her. She couldn't imagine how much worse it could really be.

"I'm sorry, this must not be an enjoyable topic for you." Lady Vera placed a hand over hers. "We don't have to talk about it."

"Thank you," she croaked, swallowing to soothe the burning in her throat.

They didn't speak anymore and settled back in comfortable silence. Still, their conversation reminded her of one more reason she needed to wrap this case up—so she could continue doing her job and help shifters in trouble. Her inner lioness seemed conflicted because it, too, had been outraged at the cruelty they'd seen, but at the same time, it her thoughts turned to the man currently hiding in the trunk, risking his own life to be here.

Panic began to form in her chest, but she calmed herself with deep, even breaths. *He's not risking his life.* Gideon knew the plan to let her take the fall should things go south. *He's just here because the queen ordered him to be and to keep them abreast of the mission.*

They continued the drive toward the Valens estate outside the city, and when the limo slowed down, Ginny looked outside and saw the towering iron gates that loomed ahead. The door to the guard shack opened and a tall, broad man in a dark gray uniform came out. He approached the driver's side first and spoke to the chauffeur, then turned to the rear passenger window.

Lady Vera lowered the glass and smiled brightly as she answered the severe-looking guard's question, who remained stony-faced. Ginny kept her hands in her lap and looked down, though when she felt the guard's gaze on her, she lifted her head and smiled shyly at him. Avoiding eye contact was a surefire way to arouse suspicion, especially if the guard was well-trained. Though he didn't return her smile, he straightened his posture and waved them forward.

Whew.

And that had been the easy part.

Ginny could see the winding road up ahead and the massive mansion in the distance. She stamped her foot three times to let Gideon know they were safely inside. He replied with three raps.

Now the real work was about to begin.

Ginny thanked her luck stars she couldn't understand Nordgensprak, but from his tone and body language, it sounded like Minister Valens was laying it on thick as he and Lady Vera enjoyed their private dinner in his richly appointed dining room.

They sat at a great oak table, lit by candlelight, as liveried servants silently and smoothly came in and out to deliver course after course as the two conversed. Or rather, Valens did most of the talking, and Lady Vera merely nodded along and replied, also managing a simper here and there. In fact, Lady Vera seemed to handle Valens so expertly that Ginny considered recruiting her to The Agency.

She shifted uncomfortably on the hard wooden chair where she sat in the corner, watching the two have dinner. The minister had welcomed them—or rather, Lady Vera, as he barely even looked at Ginny—into his luxurious home as soon as the limo pulled up to the driveway, dressed in a suit that probably cost more than what most people made in a month, reeking of some expensive designer cologne. He fawned over Lady Vera, his greedy eyes looking her up and down in a way that made Ginny's skin crawl. She vowed to finish her search here quickly, if only to ensure this smarmy, slimy creature never laid a finger on Lady Vera. Sure, Valens was handsome, rich, and charming on the surface, but Ginny couldn't help but feel that something was off about him.

Lady Vera briefly met her gaze before she replied to something Valens asked her, casually touching her own elbow. *Thank God.* That was the signal she'd been waiting for.

Valens said a few words and nodded, then stood up and helped Lady Vera out of her chair. As they passed by Ginny, she followed after them, but then let out a soft cry as she pretended to faint and crumple down to the floor.

"Greta!" Lady Vera exclaimed.

She wrapped her arms around her waist. "Hurts ... ate something ..." A stomach ache was the easiest sickness to fake, and that also meant she didn't have to memorize whole sentences of Nordgensprak.

Lady Vera spat out a string of harsh words and stamped her feet and whined.

Good girl. When they outlined their plan before coming here, Ginny told Lady Vera that while they had to sell their story to Valens, they couldn't sell it too hard. So, she needed to sound annoyed and displeased that "Greta" had gotten sick, cutting their evening short.

As Ginny lay curled up on the ground, she began to make gagging sounds as if she were going to throw. "Toilet ... please ..."

Valens harrumphed and helped her up, then led her out of the dining room. They walked down the hallway, then turned back to the main hall, then crossed over to the other side of the house. The minister pointed to the door at the end, and Ginny covered her mouth as she dashed to the bathroom.

Safely inside, she let out a sigh and pressed her ear to the door, listening to the conversation outside.

"... that stupid girl!" Lady Vera switched to English so "Greta" wouldn't be able to understand her. "I told my father we should give our servants more plain food. You know these working-class people. They're not used to the things we can afford."

"So true, my lady. I suppose we must cut our evening short. A tragedy as I really have enjoyed your company."

"Yes ... but ... we don't have to end the evening so early, do we, Oskar?"

"But your maid—"

Ginny let out louder and more exaggerating gagging sounds.

"She's already feeling poorly and is in no condition to be riding in a car. Can you imagine what would happen if she got sick in the Rolls Royce? We'd never get the smell out."

"What do you suggest, my lady?"

"Hmmm." She paused dramatically. "I'll tell her to wait there and say we cannot leave until she's fully expelled the contents of her stomach. An hour or so, just to be safe. Besides, it will finally give us some time alone," she purred.

"Excellent idea."

"Give me one moment."

Ginny stepped back and knelt in front of the toilet. A few seconds later, the door opened. "That went well!" Lady Vera whispered excitedly.

She grinned up at her. "You were great. All right, you know what to do?"

Lady Vera nodded. "I'll distract him for one hour, then come back here to fetch you."

"And if any of the servants catch me lurking about, I'll pretend I was looking for you and then faint. Then you make your apologies, berate me some more, and then we make our escape."

"Is one hour enough?"

"It'll have to be." She patted the thumb drive in her pocket. All she had to do was put it in the USB slot of any computer and once the user powered their device on, she'd be able to access it remotely. It shouldn't take more than two seconds, but finding and breaking into Valens's home office would be the hard part. From what she observed, the indoor cameras only covered the entrance and main hall, but she still had to watch out for any other staff lurking about.

A knock startled them both. "Lady Vera?" came Valens's voice. "Everything all right?"

Ginny made vomiting noises again.

"I shall be out soon, Oskar," Lady Vera called, then gave Ginny a quick side hug. "Good luck."

Ginny nodded, then turned back to the toilet and heaved just as Lady Vera opened the door. When it slammed shut behind her, she counted to sixty before getting up and straightening her outfit and wig.

All right, here we go.

Silently, she slipped out of the bathroom. From what she'd observed and from what Gideon had told her, this home was humongous. But she had to start somewhere.

Ginny crept into the room next door, which looked to be some kind of sunroom. The one after that turned out to be a library, then a drawing room, then another room filled with all kinds of paintings.

The search continued, but she still could not find

Valens's home office. However, after searching what seemed like two dozen rooms, she came upon a locked door on the east side. *This had to be it!* She made quick work of the lock and slipped inside.

Yes!

This was definitely some kind of office or study. Shelves filled with leather-bound books lined the walls, two leather wingback chairs sat next to a fireplace, and on top of a plush Persian carpet was a large heavy wooden desk with a computer monitor. Sprinting toward the desk, she crawled underneath it and saw the slim, black metal PC tower.

Hallelujah!

Taking the USB device from her pocket, she reached behind the chassis and inserted the thumb drive into a free slot. *Now all we have to do is wait for Valens to power up his computer and we'll get to see all the goodies he's been hiding.*

As she backed out of the kneehole, she misjudged the space above and her head struck the bottom of the table. "Ow!" As her hand reached up to soothe the top of her skull, she heard a strange sound as her knuckles banged on the wood. Huh. She knocked on the underside of the desk, just to make sure.

Definitely hollow.

Quickly, she got out and reached back underneath to search it, her heart hammering. Finally, her thumb brushed against what felt like a raised button just to the side. When she pressed it, she heard a *click* sound, and what had initially appeared to be a decorative panel on the apron slid out to reveal a hidden drawer.

Holy moly!

Her job was done, and the smart thing to do now was to

go back to that bathroom. But her gut screamed at her that this was something important. And so, with a deep breath, she pulled out the drawer completely.

A folder stuffed full of paper sat inside. Curious, she flipped the front open. On top was some kind of contract. She recognized the letterhead with the logo of a well-known military contractor—Blackwelle Poole. *More like mercenary*, she snorted. That particular company was on The Agency's hit list because they did business with anyone who paid their ridiculously expensive fees—including many anti-shifter groups. She thumbed through the documents, but they were in French, and she hadn't brushed up on her reading comprehension in a while, so she skimmed through it. It mostly sounded like a standard contract, though the final amount in the back nearly made her eyes pop out of her head. *Got deep pockets, huh, Minister?*

As she took the folder out of the secret drawer so she could take photos with her phone, another sheaf of papers slid out from behind the contract with the official seal of the Northern Isles on top. Thankfully, English was now an official language of the country, so Ginny was able to read it. The large, bold title made her heart jump in her throat.

Articles Introducing the Dissolution of the Monarchy.

Ginny's heart careened into her throat, but she continued on.

King Aleksei incapacitated ... Queen Sybil a foreigner ... heir to the throne not of legal age ... Dragon Guard and Dragon Navy to be disbanded ... law and order to be preserved with assistance of contractor ...

She skimmed through the rest of it, but she got the gist.

Valens was planning some kind of coup and gain control

of the government using a private military force. And he planned to start it by getting rid of King Aleksei.

The knowledge stunned her, shorting her brain for a moment. What if he'd also been working with The Knights since they had a common goal? The Knights would get rid of a powerful enemy, and Valens would be rid of the one person impeding on his trade deals. *I need to get out of here, now!*

A soft knocking sound made her jump. She nearly dropped the folders, so she clutched it tight to her chest. She'd been discovered!

"Ginny!" someone whispered. "Ginny, by the window."

Her head immediately whipped toward the windows behind the desk. There was no one out there, but then slowly, Gideon's face materialized behind a pane.

"What the hell?"

Gideon pointed to the window latch.

Idiot! She had a mind to just ignore him and leave, but she supposed he wouldn't come unless it was an emergency. *Damn it!* Reluctantly, she undid the latch.

"What are you doing here?" she hissed as Gideon lifted up the window and slid inside. "You're supposed to stay in the limo!"

"We have a problem." He dusted his hands down his pants.

"Problem? What problem?"

He nodded at the window. "That problem."

"What the—motherfucker!" she cursed when she saw the second face materialize. "What are *you* doing here?"

Stein grunted at her and by some miracle, managed to fit his bulk through the frame and climbed inside.

She glared at the colossal dragon shifter. "You're compromising this operation and—oh my God!" Her head bobbed up and down as she inspected his ill-fitting suit jacket and too-short pants. "*You* were the chauffeur."

"Yeah, sorry about that," Gideon said sheepishly. "He followed us to the Solveigson estate and insisted on coming along. Knocked out and tied up the chauffeur, so I had no choice."

"But that doesn't answer my question," she said, exasperated. "What are you doing in *here*?"

Gideon's face turned grim. "I think Valens knows you're snooping around."

"What?"

"I'm not sure what happened, but his security—"

An alarm broke out.

"He definitely knows you're prowling around in his house."

"Goddammit!" Fear replaced the outrage gripping her chest. "We had a plan! You should have stuck with it and kept your nose out of my business!" But maybe all wasn't lost. "I can still salvage this! I'll go upstairs, find his bedroom, and stuff my pockets with whatever valuables—"

A commotion from the other side of the door interrupted her. There was a shuffling of feet and a feminine cry.

"No!" Gideon hissed as he wrapped an arm around Stein, who looked about ready to explode. "You can't. Think of your duty to the king."

"Tell me where she is, you bitch!" A voice—obviously Valens—screamed.

"I don't know what you're—ow, please, Oskar, don't!"

Stein let out a furious roar that rattled Ginny's teeth and

made her lioness cower in terror. His silvery gaze burned into hers. "Do you have the evidence?"

"You're hurting me!" Lady Vera sobbed.

"Do you?" he repeated.

Rage exploded in her. "Enough to hang him."

And that seemed enough for the Dragon Guard as he flew toward the door. He practically ripped it off its hinge.

On the other side, Valens had Lady Vera pinned up to the wall, her pretty face marred by twin streaks of tears down her cheeks. His head whipped toward Stein. "Who the—"

But Valens didn't get to finish his sentence as Stein tore him away from Lady Vera and slammed him against the wall.

"Let go of me, you oaf!" Valens sputtered. "How dare you! Do you know who I am?"

Stein snarled as his massive hand wrapped around the minister's throat, making Valens freeze.

"*Loki's balls!*" Gideon cursed as they rushed toward them.

Ginny immediately went to Lady Vera and embraced her. "It's all right. You're fine," she soothed as she continued to sob. "You did good."

"He ... he ... went out of the room. I didn't realize he'd gone to check on you," Lady Vera hiccupped. "I tried ... did everything to stop him, even try to kiss him."

Stein let out a growl and began to squeeze the minister's throat. Valens yelped and clawed at the Dragon Guard's hand, but it was no use.

"Stein, don't kill him," Gideon said.

"Give me one good reason—"

The sound of approaching footsteps thundered from

down the hall interrupted him. Stein cursed and loosened his grip, but didn't let go.

"Oh, crap!" Ginny groaned as she saw the dozen or so men dressed in guard uniforms were running toward them, weapons raised.

Gideon darted in front of them and lifted his hand. "Stop!" he commanded. "In the name of the crown, stop!"

The men immediately halted in their tracks, but looked at each other, confused.

"I am Gideon of the Dragon Guards. By order of His Majesty, King Aleksei, Ruler of the Northern Isles, I am arresting Oskar Valens for treason. Put your weapons down and lie facedown on the ground now, or you, too, will be charged with aiding and abetting a traitor." Thankfully, all of them followed his order.

Fishing his phone from his pocket, Gideon tapped on the screen. "I'm going to call His Majesty."

CHAPTER 11

Gideon pressed his lips together. From behind the one-way mirror, he watched Chief Inspector Hadon interrogate Valens in an interview room at the Ministry Police Department. Ginny stood beside him, silent as he was, but he could see the tension in her body. But then again, he felt just as anxious. In fact, the atmosphere was dark and tense, and he could also sense the unease from the two other occupants of the room—King Aleksei and Queen Sybil.

Still, Ginny's chilly demeanor and silence perturbed him. She hadn't spoken a word to him since they left Valens's office, and that had been a couple of hours ago. She'd obviously been outraged that he had intervened in her operation, but what was he supposed to do when he saw the minister's security team converging on the house? His gut and his dragon told him that something was *very* wrong and that it was overkill to have two dozen men in combat gear going after one thieving maid.

Obviously, he'd been right. Valens knew if his plans to

overthrow King Aleksei had been discovered, that was the end for him.

From the moment they arrested him, Valens's disposition had swung from vehement indignation as they hauled him away to the police headquarters to a calm smugness when they brought him into the drab room. In fact, he'd been so confident, he waived away his right to legal counsel. When the chief inspector arrived, he looked as cool as a cucumber, but once all the evidence had been presented to him, the facade crumbled, and he folded like a cheap lawn chair, bawling and begging for mercy.

Chief Hadon pushed a folder toward Valens. "And with this evidence we found, we were able to connect your transactions to pay off Blackwelle Poole using illicit funds from gemstones stolen from the royal mines."

Valens's complexion turned even sicklier.

Queen Sybil gasped. "Did you know something about this, Aleksei?"

The king glared harder at Valens. "I was informed of the theft a few months ago, but I let the police handle the matter." His thumb and forefinger massaged his temple. "I just never thought the gemstones would be used in an attempt to overthrow me."

Hadon continued. "We even have CCTV video of you during your clandestine meeting with the executives of Blackwelle in Venice." Planting his hands on the table, he leaned forward. "Clever of you, utilizing the tour as cover."

Thank you, Shifter Protection Agency. From the phone data and messages they had copied from Valens's phone, The Agency was able to track down his whereabouts on the day of the attack. They tracked his phone location data as he traveled to Torcello and then found footage of him a meeting with a representative of Blackwelle at the Church of Maria Assunta from a security camera from an antique store across the street.

"Will you confess, then, Minister Valens?" Chief Hadon asked, eyes narrowing. "To your crimes? The judge may be more merciful and consider taking the death penalty off the table."

"I—d-d-death penalty?" Valens sputtered. "But I committed no grave crime! I confess to stealing the gem stones and planning the dissolution of the monarchy, but no one was harmed!"

"You attempted to assassinate our king!" Hadon bellowed. "If King Aleksei had not survived the attack in Venice, we would not even be speaking now."

"B-b-but I did not ... that wasn't me ... I ..."

"Wasn't you?" Hadon scoffed. "You wrote it on those articles yourself. Once the king was incapacitated—"

"I wasn't going to kill him!" Valens shot back. "Just poison him with enough bloodsbane to knock him out for a few days. Please!" Turning to the mirror, he lunged forward, getting on his knees, hands clamped together. "Y-Your Majesty, if you're there ... listening to me ... I swear I had nothing to do with your assassination attempt!"

Hadon grabbed him by the shoulders and forced him backwards. "Enough!"

"Have mercy, please!" Valens screamed.

"Calm down or I'll have to take you away to a cell," Hadon threatened.

The minister sank back down on the chair, planted his

elbows on the table, and buried his face in his hands. "Call my lawyer, please."

"I've heard enough," King Aleksei growled, and slammed his palm on the button next to the window to mute the speakers. "My father and I have always had our differences with Valens, but I never thought he'd do this."

Queen Sybil rose from her chair, planted herself in front of the mirror, then glared at Valens. "He's a creep, I just knew he was up to no good. He's a politician, after all. *Argh!* I want to burn him to ashes. Can I do that, Aleksei? Please, can I? I promise I'll make him hurt."

Her mate gave her a sad smile. "I have no doubt you could. But he is still a citizen of the Northern Isles and thus has his rights."

The queen pursed her lips. "Fine. I guess we'll have to let justice do its work."

"And thanks to you, Ginny, we have all the evidence we need to convict him." King Aleksei gave her a quick nod.

"It was my job, Your Majesty," she replied. "Happy to be of service. And of course, I couldn't have done it all alone. Lady Vera should take half the credit at least."

"Ah, of course, I will let her know my deepest thanks and gratitude for her service."

"Oh dear, I'll visit her in the morning," Queen Sybil said. "She was so distraught after we went to see the royal physician."

"How is she, Your Majesty?" Gideon asked, concerned.

The queen sighed sadly. "Shaken up. But hearing the news that the evidence she helped obtain could convict Valens will surely cheer her up."

"I am glad you were there," King Aleksei said to Gideon. "But tell me, how did Stein end up in Valens's mansion?"

"Yes, about that." He scratched at the back of his head. "He basically ambushed me at the Solveigson estate. Knocked out the driver before I could say anything, so unless I wanted to play chauffeur, I had to let him drive. We were waiting inside the limo—thankfully the heat sensing cameras were only located along the outside walls of the property—when we saw the guards gathering and storming up to the house. Stein, uh, insisted we investigate." Actually, the other Dragon Guard pretty much just told him 'I'm heading in' and stormed off. "Turns out, Valens went to check on Ginny and knew something was up when she wasn't in the bathroom."

King Aleksei blew out a breath. "I just hope Stein's calmed down enough by morning. Rorik had to drag him into the old dungeons because he wouldn't stop threatening to castrate and disembowel Valens."

Queen Sybil gave him a cryptic smile which he returned with a raised brow, indicating they were communicating privately.

"Well then." King Aleksei cleared his throat. "It is late. Past midnight. We should head back and retire. You two have surely earned some rest." *And if you need a day off to be alone with your mate, just make sure Rorik knows*, the king quipped.

He grinned at the king. "Goodnight, Your Majesties."

The royal couple left the room, and once they were alone, he turned to Ginny. "We should get going, too."

She didn't move, her gaze fixed on Valens, who sat alone in the interview room.

He shoved his fingers through his hair. "Look, I understand that you're mad about me and Stein coming in, but what was I supposed to do? Just let those men find you and shoot you?" The thought made him and his dragon seethe with rage, but Ginny continued to give him the silent treatment. "And given the chance, I would do it again because you're my—"

"I could have handled it!" she exploded. "I had a plan."

"It's done. Everything worked out."

"You shouldn't have been there in the first place!"

"And then what? Wait around the palace, then receive word that you'd been pumped full of bullets? Or worse, discovered your and Lady Vera's bodies dumped somewhere? Valens realized something was wrong, and he knew that evidence he kept was damning. He was backed into a corner and wouldn't have hesitated to take both your lives to save his."

Her lips clamped together, but her eyes blazed.

"Don't you understand, Ginny? No one could stop me from trying to protect you, not even you yourself!" The raw, tightness in his chest refused to go away, not when the thought of what could have happened to her opened a flood of emotions in him. "I would do anything to save you, even if I had to sacrifice myself. You're my—"

"No!"

"Ginny—" He tried to grip her arms, but she back away, pressing herself against the one-way glass window. "Ginny, what's the matter?"

There was that vacant stare in her eyes again; it passed briefly, but he'd seen it.

"We're done here," she declared.

"Done?" Now that enraged him and his dragon. "We're not done. We'll never be done. You're—"

"Shut up!" She held a hand up. "I'm leaving now. Back to the palace. A-and tomorrow, The Agency is sending a plane to get me."

He suddenly realized what she *really* meant, and his dragon recoiled at the denial of their mating bond. "No," he said in an oddly calm voice. "You're not stepping foot on that plane."

She managed a contemptuous laugh. "And you're going to stop me? Last I heard, this was a free—"

He was on her fast, gripping her arms tight and pushing her against the window. But he was finished with this nonsense. "You're mine," he growled. "My mate. You know that. Why are you trying to deny it?"

"You never said anything either," she shot back.

"That was before. And this is now. After what happened between us—"

"Please. It was sex, nothing more."

He leaned close to her, so close he could feel the warmth of her body. "It was more than that. You felt it."

"Let. Go. Of me." Sky-blue eyes blazed up at him.

"What's this really about, Ginny? Why deny the bond between us?"

"I can't stay here. You *know* that."

"Why not?"

"I-I have a job. My duty. You should understand that most of all."

"That's bullshit and not what I'm talking about. You can still do your job *and* be my mate. People compromise for relationships all the time." God, why did it feel like she was slipping through his fingers?

Her lower lip trembled. "I don't want to compromise! I want to leave!"

Those words struck him deep. And so, he let his grip on her slacken. "All right. That's all you had to say." His dragon let out a deep howl of despair, but he shut it down and locked it away.

She reached out to him, but dropped her hand halfway. With a sharp intake of breath, she stepped aside and headed toward the exit.

It wasn't until he heard the slamming of the door that it felt really final. *You should understand most of all*, she said.

He did, he really did. But his mistake was in wishing that he'd been worth it to stay anyway. But no, he wasn't worth it, not even for her.

What did you expect? His own mother abandoned him, and he was her own blood and flesh. Yet, she left without a single glance back. Why would a mate be any different?

Never fall in love, Gideon. It's not worth it.

The memory of that day was so clear in his mind. The smell of fresh-cut grass. The warmth of the bright morning sun. His father's hand as he squeezed his shoulder. The shadow of his dragon as it loomed over him before flying away.

That was the last time Gideon had seen him.

It felt like he'd been there forever, just standing there, unable to move even one centimeter. His dragon cried out in despair, begging him to go after her.

"She doesn't want us!" he howled at his animal. It

cowered and hung its head limply, then slunk back into a corner.

He scrubbed a hand down his face. There was nothing he could do now. Just head home and go on with his life. So, he left the interview room and walked out of the Ministry Police headquarters. His thoughts began to turn to Ginny, wondering how she got back to the palace, but he shut that down as even that made his throat tighten.

He spotted the well-manicured lawn across the driveway and decided to shift there. As he jogged down the steps of the building, he saw a car parked at the bottom. The rear lid was popped open, a figure was bent over, searching through the trunk, a tire jack on the ground.

"Excuse me, do you need help? Oh—it's you. What are you doing—*ack*!" He slapped at his neck as he felt a painful prick. "Are you ..." A strange kind of weakness came over him, then he felt his legs give under him as he was pushed into the trunk.

And then the world went dark.

CHAPTER 12

Ginny placed the sweatshirt into her backpack, then zipped it closed. In truth, she had barely unpacked anyway, so there wasn't much to put away. With a long, deep sigh, she sank back on the bed. A glance over at the clock on the nightstand told her that she'd have to leave for the airport in an hour.

Her lioness let out a sad yowl. She shut her eyes, not even having the strength to berate it, not when she hadn't slept all night.

I did the right thing.

Walking out of that room last night had been the hardest thing Ginny had ever done. Her lioness, for one, didn't make it easy, fighting and clawing at her in every way. But she had to do it. She had to leave before she broke down and crawled back to him and begged him to take her back. To let him know she didn't mean any of those things she said. That heartbreaking expression on his face made something fracture inside of her.

But with his own words, he lit up every single fear receptor in her brain.

I would do anything to save you, even if I had to sacrifice myself.

She would never let that happen. Not again. She'd already decided to leave once the case was done, anyway. The events of last night had only solidified her decision. No one would sacrifice their life for her ever again. It had been painful enough with Kristos, but Gideon? Her already broken soul would be reduced to nothing.

Pain gripped her chest, crushing her lungs until she could barely breathe. Bounding up to her feet, she grabbed her backpack and slung it over her shoulder. She had hoped to say goodbye to Sybil, and maybe even Poppy or Alric, but she had to get out of here *now*.

As she dashed out of the room, she collided into someone tall and broad. Her heart leapt for a moment as strong hands gripped her, and she stared up into deep amber eyes, but just like each time she bumped into Niklas, she knew it wasn't *him*.

Shock crossed his face as he glanced down at her back-pack. "So, it's true."

She looked up at him, defiant. "Yes. I solved the case. Found your mole. It's time for me to—hey!" Niklas crowded her back into the room. "What the hell?"

"I thought I misheard the queen when she said you were leaving. Why? Tell me, what did my brother do?"

"Nothing."

"I'm going to smack him upside the head until he says sorry and begs you to stay."

"I told you, he didn't do anything! I'm leaving, and my decision is final."

"Wait." He held a finger up. "Are you telling me you dumped *him*?"

Her nostrils flared. "I did not dump him. We weren't even a thing—"

"You're mates!"

"How did you—"

"It doesn't matter! Why the hell are you leaving?"

He paced back and forth, shoving his fingers into his hair in a way that reminded her of Gideon. It made her heart ache, but she pushed those feelings aside. "I have a job. With The Agency. There are so many of our kind out there who need our help and—" She shrieked as Niklas lunged toward her, grabbed her backpack and tossed it away. "You can't stop me!"

"Oh yes, I can. Now." He crossed his arms over his chest. "Tell me the real reason why you're leaving us?"

"That is the real reason! You know what it's like to have a job—"

"That's bullshit," he shot back. "Gideon would follow you to the ends of the earth if you asked him to! Gods know I would for my mate. He would do anything for you. Die for you and—"

"I don't want him to die!" The words flew out of her mouth before she could stop them. She gasped and covered her mouth.

His jaw hardened, and his gaze turned steely. "You don't think you're already killing him in a way, walking out on him like this? A man can only be abandoned so many times before he loses his spirit."

Abandoned so many times?

Niklas lowered his hands to his side and relaxed his shoulders. "I see."

"See what?"

"He hasn't told you ... of course not." He scrubbed his hand down his face. "Why would he?"

"Tell me what?"

"Look, Ginny, I'm not telling you this to make you pity Gideon, but you should understand. What happened to him ... to us."

There was a phantom pain there that echoed on that familiar face. She'd seen it before—last night before she walked out of that room.

Niklas continued. "Our parents ... they didn't have a happy marriage. My mother is from one of the noble families here, a Jarl's daughter. Marrying into the House of Aumont had been her father's wish, a great honor to their family, especially if she were to bear the house more dragon sons. And so she did. She had us. I think ... I think she was content for a time, but she had these romantic notions, and my father wasn't exactly the most affectionate type. But he loved her so much he did everything he could to make her happy. Even let her have lovers on the side."

"What?" Ginny curled her hands into fists.

"Yeah. She was ... something." He winced, but continued. "One day, she decides that wasn't enough. And so, she told my father she was leaving to go and live in Europe with one of her beaus—an Italian count or whatever—and she left."

A hollow feeling crept into her stomach. "She just left?"

He nodded. "Just walked out the door. Didn't even say goodbye or give me and Gideon so much as a backward glance while we sat on the stairs, watching my father get on his knees and beg her to stay."

Oh, Gideon. She closed her eyes, almost imagining the sight of the two twin boys watching their mother leave them.

"My father was never really the same after that. He drank a lot. Hung on there for a good year or so until the accident." His voice had choked up at the end, and Ginny didn't say anything so he could compose himself. "We were out playing on the lawn, and I saw him stumble out of the house. Gideon had been so happy to see him out of bed that he ran toward him. I remember seeing him kneel down, whisper something to Gideon, then pat him on the head before he shifted and flew off." Niklas's lower lip trembled. "They said it was an accident. He had so much alcohol in his system he didn't burn it off in time. They think he passed out while flying and—"

"It's okay." Reaching out, she cupped his cheek. "You don't have to say any more."

Niklas brushed his fingers at the corner of his eye. "I just want you to understand. So you can—"

A ringing sound interrupted them as her phone vibrated in her pocket. Oh, she wanted to hug Niklas right now, but she feared that she would start sobbing if she did. So instead, she picked up the call.

"Hello?" she sniffed.

"Ms. Ginevra, it is me, Nepheli Kritikos," came the heavily-accented voice through the speakers.

"Nepheli? What is it?"

"Ms. Ginevra, did you get the last email I sent you?"

"Email? About what? Is it my next mission?"

"No, no. About the Northern Isles case."

"Northern—Oh, Nepheli, didn't they tell you? That case is solved. We found the mole."

"I see. But still, I think you should read it and my findings. Please, it is important."

Ginny remembered Nepheli as no-nonsense, hyper-focused, and whip-smart. It was what made her a great analyst. "All right. I'll check it now." She shrugged and hung up, then opened her inbox and glossed over its contents.

"What. The. Fuck."

"Ginny?" Niklas cocked his head to the side. "Are—"

"Shh!" What Nepheli wrote didn't quite make sense, so she read through it again.

Ms. Ginevra,

Apologies it has taken me a while to send you the background check on the final subject. I had to verify multiple times that the information was correct and there was no fault or double hits on the name and birthdate.

I'm attaching the documents for your perusal, obtained directly from the Northern Isles official census. You can see that the name, parents' names, and birthdate match those in both the birth and death certificate. And so, unless there was a clerical error, I can tell you without a doubt that subject Melina Gunnarson is in fact, deceased.

I took the liberty of contacting her next of kin, her mother. Please find attached a photo of Ms. Gunnarson. Perhaps it might prove useful in finding the correct Ms. Gunnarson.

Nepheli Kritikos

Her fingers shook as she tapped the files and skimmed through them. Her heart hammered as she moved on to the attached photo.

"Holy fuck!"

"What the hell is going on?" Niklas said, exasperated.

Suddenly it all clicked into place—not all of it because she still didn't have a motive—but enough anyway to form a clearer picture in her head. "I knew it!"

"Knew what?"

She'd been so angry at Gideon last night and then consumed with fear that she ignored her gut and what it was trying to tell her as she watched Valens's interrogation. "I don't think Valens is your mole."

"What are you saying? You saw the evidence—hell, you found it and helped put the guy away."

"Yes, but ..." She needed to think. Piece her thoughts together. "Don't you think it's weird?"

"What's weird?"

"That Valens confessed to everything else—except the Venice attack."

Niklas's golden brows knitted together. "Really?"

"Yes. The moment he saw all the evidence against him, he sang like a canary. Probably realized he was done for." And why he'd been furious when he realized Ginny was gone and Lady Vera was obviously trying to distract him. *Gideon had been right about Valens being backed into a corner.* And then she would have been killed *and* responsible for Lady Vera's death if he and Stein hadn't been there.

"Ginny?"

She mentally shook her head. "Valens admitted to the theft of the gemstones, hiring Blackwelle Poole, meeting with them, and conspiring to incapacitate Aleksei and dissolve the monarchy."

He snorted distastefully. "Can you imagine what he'd be like as a ruler? He'd run us into the ground."

"See, that's it. I managed to skim those papers he drew up. He wasn't planning on being king or dictator or whatever. The articles of dissolution proposed an elected parliament. And now this." She shoved her phone in his face.

"What is 'this'?" he asked impatiently.

"Our analyst sent me some documents to prove that Melina Gunnarson is dead."

"She died? Oh no! Why didn't anyone say anything? And I just saw her last night, leaving the queen's office really late."

"No, no, dragon brain!" she said, exasperated. Zooming in on the death certificate, she enlarged the date. "See? She passed away five years ago. Mountain climbing accident. And look." She swiped to the photo, showing a blonde, blue-eyed beauty. "That's the real Melina Gunnarson."

"Then who's been working with the queen?"

"That's what we need to find out. C'mon, let's go see Queen Sybil."

They headed to the royal apartments and luckily, King Aleksei was there too. Ginny explained everything to the couple, including all the evidence Nepheli had gathered.

"What does this have to do with Valens being the mole?" King Aleksei asked.

"He's not," Ginny said. Her gut had screamed it at her, so she had to say it. "I mean, I think Melina—or whoever she is —is your mole."

"And Valens and his plan to overthrow the monarchy?" Sybil added.

"Pure coincidence. Oh, he's guilty as fuck of those other crimes, all right. But not of being your mole. Melina is."

Sybil cradled her forehead with her hand. "I can't believe it."

"At the very least, we should investigate Melina," Niklas suggested. "If it's a clerical error, then we can get it cleared up."

"All right." The queen got up. "I'll have her files sent to me and comb through them myself."

"For now, we must act normally," King Aleksei said in a calm voice. "Because we don't want to accuse her if it's just a misunderstanding or alarm her and send her fleeing."

"Or have her go crazy, like Valens," Ginny added.

"I shall gather the rest of the Dragon Guard so they can be informed of these new developments." King Aleksei closed his eyes, seemingly calling his loyal guards through their mind link.

Ginny sat down on the couch next to the queen as they waited for everyone to arrive. She hadn't expected she'd be seeing Gideon so soon or at all, but she could act normal if he could. Her lioness on the other hand ... well, it was confused at the turn of events, and sensing Ginny was shoring up her mental defenses for when he did walk into that door, it seemed anxious but excited.

They waited in silence, tension rising in the room by degrees. Stein had been waiting just outside, so he came in as soon as the king called him. His usual stony-faced demeanor was so different from the beast she'd seen last night. She had no doubt he really would have torn Valens apart piece by piece and enjoyed every minute of it. A few minutes later, Rorik joined them.

It was like god was punishing her or something, as she waited on tenterhooks for Gideon to appear. They all sat down, watching the door for his appearance.

"Is Gideon occupied?" The king asked Rorik.

He shook his head. "I did not assign him any duties today, Your Majesty. What did he say when you called him through our mind link?"

King Aleksei blinked. "Actually, I just realized he did not answer me."

From out of nowhere, a ball of dread started to form in Ginny's stomach. She swallowed, trying to ignore it.

Niklas frowned. "He's not answering."

"Is he out of range?" Sybil asked, then her gaze flickered to Ginny briefly. "Maybe he, um, needed to be alone."

"He wouldn't just leave the palace without telling me or anyone," Niklas reasoned.

A silence passed over them, then King Aleksei shook his head. "No, Stein, I don't think he's just asleep."

The Dragon Guard grunted in response.

The king continued. "I'm sure he's all right. Why don't you go check his room, Niklas? Rorik, call the palace security team and ask them if they've seen him anywhere."

The two left, and as the minutes ticked by, the dread in Ginny's belly grew.

"We'll find him," Sybil assured her. "Not that he's missing. Or anything like that."

"I ... I just left him, last night. Chief Hadon had one of his constables drive me back to the palace." Her head buzzed, and all she could think of was Gideon. Her lioness, too, began to stalk back and forth, tail whipping nervously.

"I can't find him!" Niklas said, bursting through the door. "I've asked around, and no one has seen him since yesterday. And I can't find Melina either. She's not in her office. I saw her last night leaving the palace by herself."

"What? But there's no reason for her to work late." The

queen shot up and stalked to the phone on the console table by the door. "Hello, can you put me through to Ms. Gunnarson?" she said into the receiver.

A heartbeat passed, and when Ginny saw the crestfallen expression on Sybil's face, her stomach dropped. The queen didn't have to say anything.

Ginny knew something was very, very wrong.

CHAPTER 13

Gideon felt the pain as if it had been lodged right into his very bones. It overwhelmed him, making it difficult to move or think. Something roared inside him.

His dragon.

The creature urged him to fight the pain and the darkness. To break free. *Fight.*

I'm too weak. Hurts.

His dragon whined, nosing at him to get up. To escape.

Escape?

But he couldn't see anything. Couldn't even feel anything. It was like he'd been suspended in a vat of tar, unable to tell which way was up or down. And the pain. Gods, the pain. He didn't want to feel it anymore, so he let the darkness take him again.

When he came to again, the pain had mellowed to a mild discomfort. He couldn't move, and his body felt hot and feverish, as if he'd been fighting some infection. It was something he hadn't experienced in a long time, maybe back when he was a child and his dragon hadn't fully matured yet. But at least the pain was gone.

Slowly, he opened his eyes. His vision was blurry, but he could smell grease and oil. Then he remembered what happened.

Why did Melina Gunnarson drug him and put him in the trunk of her car?

The vehicle went over a large bump, and Gideon's head hit the ceiling of the trunk with a loud thud. However, that seemed to have woken up his brain. Fight, his dragon had said. His body still felt weak. What had Melina given him? Bloodsbane? He'd studied the substance before, and they never mentioned any kind of pain. How long had he been out?

The automobile slowed down, and he relaxed. Well, he was wide awake now, but he couldn't move. But once he did regain control of his body, he could easily overpower Melina. He would pretend to still be drugged and could play that to his advantage for now.

The engine stopped, and a car door opened. He held his breath waiting for Melina to come and get him out of the trunk. But moments passed and nothing happened. Instead, he heard several voices outside. Focusing his hearing, he listened in on the conversation.

"... glad to see you have succeeded."

"Of course," Melina sneered. "Did you have any doubts I would, General Harris?"

"I must admit, I was disappointed when our attack on the Northern Isles failed two years ago. But I see planting you as a backup plan paid off. You've worked your way up the palace ranks in such a short time."

"It was so easy," Melina scoffed. "I've been training for five years for this undercover operation. And I just happened to find the right identity to take over."

Gideon realized that Melina had been speaking in English and had completely lost her Northern Isles accent. *Bastards.* So, The Knights had somehow snuck in Melina—or whoever she was—into the country while everyone was focused on fighting the attackers two years ago.

"And so once again, General, I'm here to save the day." Melina knocked on the trunk of the car. "Thanks to your men's stupidity, we lost our chance to be rid of the dragon king in Venice. I can't believe how incompetent your men are. I gave you the perfect opportunity to strike and you flub it up."

"I did not flub it up," the general shot back, indignant. "We did not count on the queen."

"Well, you should have! She breathes fire, for God's sake, what did you think would happen? Did you underestimate her because she's a woman?" She let out a disgusted grunt. "At least you got to test out the new serum on that pesky Dragon Guard. Formula X-82 seemed to have prevented him from healing that knife wound quickly. And he still felt weak for a few days after that."

"Many of our other subjects died, but I suppose our operative did not hit deep enough for the formula to make its way to the major organs. And it worked in subduing the second guard?"

"He's sleeping like a baby in the trunk."

Gideon gritted his teeth. So, the poison they used on Niklas and him—this Formula X-82—was some kind of serum that could incapacitate or even kill shifters. But why kidnap him?

"Excellent," General Harris said. "Our scientists will be pleased. With this dragon as our test subject, they'll be able to perfect the formula, and maybe we can finally be rid of these creatures."

So that's why Melina needed him alive. So they could use him as a lab rat. *Need to escape now.* But his body was still too feeble. He doubted he even had enough strength to fly, much less shift. Somehow, he had to try.

"We should leave, before anyone discovers he's gone."

"Finally. I've been wanting to get off this island for years."

Gideon prepared himself mentally as he heard the lid pop open. He shut his eyes tight, the brightness outside nearly blinding him. Morning already? He didn't realize he'd been out for hours.

"I know you're awake, you disgusting creature," General Harris spat. "Take him."

Two pairs of meaty hands grabbed him and hauled him out. He landed on his knees, but he ignored the pain that shot up his thighs as he gathered his thoughts. Think!

"Take him to the boats so we can rendezvous with the sub."

Submarine. *Clever.* Because the attack two years ago had exposed their location to The Knights, they had shored up their air defenses, but as far as Gideon knew, they still relied on patrols by the Royal Dragon Navy to protect their waters.

The two men dragged him from the road, down through a

rocky path before reaching the black sand beach. He lifted his head and saw three rubber boats on the shore.

It was now or never, but his body remained uncooperative.

Gideon!

What the—

Gideon!

It was Niklas! He was reaching out through their mental link, which meant he was in range.

Niklas, I'm here! On a beach somewhere. She drugged me and kidnapped me—

Melina, right? She's the mole.

How did you know?

His twin chuckled. *How else? Your mate figured it out. Ginny's about ready to beat the shit out of her, and I'm very tempted to let her because you know, I don't hit women and stuff.*

Ginny? But she should be long gone by now.

There! I think I see her car. Hold on, we're coming to get you.

Niklas wait! There's something you should know. She's not alone. He quickly explained to Niklas about the general and the submarine. *We need to stop them before they get away. But I don't know how many of them there are. And I'm too weak. Don't think I can shift. Call the others.*

All right, you hold tight, bro. The cavalry is on the way.

I'll try to delay them. Gideon breathed an inner sigh of relief. All he had to do was wait for the rest of the Dragon Guard to come. The feeling was starting to return to his body, so he began to struggle.

"The hell?" one of his captors cursed.

"What's going on?" General Harris barked. "Secure him! But don't kill him!"

Ah, just what he needed to know. They needed him alive. So, he dug his heels into the black sand and fought against his captors with all his might.

Fight, his dragon urged. *Fight!*

"You imbeciles!" Melina shouted. "Stop fucking around and get him on the boat!"

His strength was not up to full capacity but he managed to kick one of the men in the shins, sending him howling as he let go of Gideon's right arm. The second man, however, wrestled him into the ground, shoving his face in the sand before the first man somehow managed to kick him in the chin with a heavy booted foot. It sent his head snapping back, spots appearing before his eyes. *Niklas*, he reached out. *Please tell me they're here.*

Er, sort of?

He heard a loud, animalistic roar in the distance, then the pounding of paws on sand. When his vision cleared, the sight before him made his heart spring into his throat.

It was a lioness, leaping out from the craggy rocks. The sleek lines of its muscled body carried a grace that belied its power. It appeared to fly, like an avenging angel, before it landed on the man who kicked him. He let out a blood-curdling scream as the animal raked its claws down his body.

Mine, his dragon roared.

Ginny?

He'd been so entranced, and frankly confused, by her appearance that it took him a second to realize the he was now being dragged into one of the boats. The roar of the engine starting deafened his ears.

Must. Fight. Whatever this Formula X-82 was, it was strong. No wonder Niklas had nearly died. But he had to keep trying. Ginny's lioness had been determined to save him, and so, he wasn't going down without a fight.

CHAPTER 14

G inny's lioness roared with fury as it sank its claws into the puny human who dared hurt their mate. Blinded with rage, it sought revenge. Blood flooded into its mouth as it went straight for the jugular, sharp teeth easily breaking skin and flesh.

Grit and determination and sheer perseverance had gotten her this far. When they confirmed that Melina kidnapped Gideon based on the security footage from the Ministry Police headquarters, they immediately sprang into action.

More traffic cams caught Melina's car as it headed out of Odelia, but once it reached the central highway where there were no more cameras, they had to split up. The main island wasn't very big, and its major highway could only go east or west. Rorik flew west, and Niklas and Ginny went east. Once Niklas got in contact with Gideon through their mental link, they landed by Melina's car, called Stein back at the palace, and came up with the plan—Niklas would capture the submarine, and she would save Gideon. When she saw that man kick Gideon, however, her animal had gone crazy and now it seemed hell bent to extract the maximum amount of pain on the man who hurt their mate.

He needs us! she pleaded with her lioness.

Finally, it listened and lifted its head from the bloody carnage. Sure enough, the other captor was now dragging Gideon into one of the rubber boats. The lioness turned and ran toward the shore.

Ginny's heart slammed against her rib cage as she saw the violent, churning waves crash against the sand, and they halted. The foamy waters hypnotized her as fear gripped her entire body, making her and her lioness unable to move. The bad memories flooded her brain, and she couldn't breathe. The water. Getting into her nostrils and mouth. Filling her lungs. Kristos's face as it disappeared into the murky depths.

No!

It was her lioness, screaming at her.

Mine!

Oh God! Gideon!

The boat's engine roared as it sped away. Ginny snapped herself out of the trance and then quickly shifted back into human form. She and her lion were of the same mind. They knew what they had to do to save their mate.

She ran to the remaining boat and kicked the engine on. It shot forward, and she hung on for dear life as the momentum slammed her back. She pushed the boat to its limits until she caught up to Gideon's captors.

Her eyes widened as she got closer. Gideon knocked the other man over, sending him into the ocean. However, Melina jumped on his back, and they struggled before they, too, fell over the side.

"No!" she screamed. Adrenaline surged into her system, and without a second thought, she jumped off the side and into the dark, icy waters.

No, no, no, no! Not again. She couldn't let him die. *I love him.* It was a shitty time to admit it, but the words just popped into her brain.

She kicked and dove, trying to find any sign of him. *Please, please.* She had to find him. Or she might as well drown too, because she would never be able to live without him.

Her lungs burned, but she continued to search. Suddenly, something shiny appeared below her. Glowing. No, sparkling.

What the—

Ginny wasn't sure what happened, but one moment, she was drowning in the salty ocean and the next, air rushed into her as she shot out of the water like a rocket. Long, scaly arms held her tight, and when she opened her eyes, she saw only the blue sky and her cheek was pressed against leathery scales. *Gideon!*

Her lioness purred with delight, and his dragon answered with a deep, satisfied rumble.

As quickly as they flew up, they began to descend. Ginny screamed as they landed—no, crashed on the shore. Thankfully, the dragon flipped over in time, so she just bounced across its scaly belly before landing on the soft black sand.

"Ugh." The wind got knocked out of her, but the moment she gathered her thoughts, she scrambled to her feet. Relief washed over her as she saw the dragon slowly shrink and transform back into its human form.

"Gideon! Oh God, Gideon!" She flew to him, wrapping

her arms around him. "I thought ... I thought I'd lost you," she sobbed into his chest.

"Can ... breathe ..."

"Oh! Sorry!" She released him, but crawled up to cradle his face in her hands. "Are you okay? Do you need mouth-to-mouth?"

He shook his head, then stared up at her with those gorgeous amber orbs. "I said I *can* breathe," he rasped. "Underwater."

"What?" she exclaimed, pulling away. He let out a pained groan when his head landed on the sand. "Sorry!"

"I'm ... fine." He winced as he braced himself up on one elbow. "Melina ... sorry to say, was not so lucky," he spat, then bit out a string of Nordgensprak that didn't sound like he was sorry at all.

"But what do you mean you can breathe underwater?" Her mind was still processing it.

"I ... was trying to tell you that when I took you to my secret spot the other day. Water dragons can breathe underwater. You didn't have to—" He stopped short, his face turning blank, before his mouth parted and his eyes widened. "You thought I was drowning."

"Yes," she whispered.

"Oh, *pusen* ..." Reaching out, he cupped the side of her face. "I'm sorry."

"No, I'm sorry. I shouldn't have pushed you away." She swallowed the lump in her throat. Would he ever forgive her for abandoning him, like his mother did?

"I should have—I didn't realize it then, but I do now. Your old partner, he died trying to save you. And your fear of the water ... I was insensitive."

"I guess I don't have to worry about you drowning." But the joke fell flat. "I mean—"

"Ginny, I will always protect you, no matter what. I'm afraid that's not something you control or stop. I love you too much."

She sucked in a breath. "You do?"

"Yes, of course. But if you feel ... if you feel you can't be with me. To live here in the Northern Isles and compromise, I understand." He swallowed audibly. "I want what's best for you. What will make you happy. If that means letting you go, then so be it."

She was speechless. He was giving her an out. She could leave and travel and be an agent and never have to risk being hurt.

But then again, she would never see Gideon's smile or those gorgeous dimples. Or hear his laugh. Or catch that look of concentration on his face while he read. Or kiss those lips or— "I love you. I really do. And I want to stay."

Now it was his turn to run out of words. But he didn't have to say anything as she saw joy in those bright amber eyes. "Ginny—*oomph!*"

She laughed as she launched herself at him, knocking him down and plastering herself on top of his body. Her mouth found his, kissing his lips with all the love and happiness she could muster.

And then it happened. She thought the surf had somehow reached them, but it was something else that washed over them. A warmth that covered them both before slowly pulling away like the waves returning to the ocean. Except once it was gone, it left behind one being. Two bodies, but a single soul.

"Ginny," he whispered against her mouth. "Did you—"

"Yes." Her lioness cried with joy as it felt the oneness with their mate. The bond had formed. "Yes, I did. Gideon." She gently cupped the sides of his face. "Silly boy. I'm never going to leave you. Never ever. You'll never be rid of me."

"As if I would try." He reached up to pull her down, but a large, deafening crash made them both start and scramble apart. "What the hell?"

A blue-green water dragon crawled out of the ocean, its claws digging into the sand as its lower body wrapped around what appeared to be a 100-foot submarine. It dragged the sub completely out of the water, then released it before slithering over to Ginny and Gideon.

"Hey, guys," Niklas said as he transformed back into his human form. "What did I miss?"

Realizing she was as naked as the day she was born—as she'd left her clothes by Melina's car when she took them off before shifting into her lioness form—Ginny hid her body behind Gideon.

"Not much." Gideon grinned down at her. And through their bond, she could feel all the love, excitement, and strangely enough, contentment from him. "Looks like you've been busy yourself." He nodded at the submarine.

"Yeah, well, someone's gotta come to the rescue, right?" He tsked and shook his head. "But it seems like you're the one who gets the girl, though."

"Excuse me? *I* did the rescuing too," Ginny shot back. "Did you see me take that motherfucker down?"

"And you definitely got the girl—er, guy," Gideon added.

She smirked up at him. "That, I did."

CHAPTER 15

"So, do you come here often?"

Gideon couldn't help the smile he felt spreading across his lips as he heard the familiar voice of his mate. But he kept his head down and eyes on the page of the book in his hand. "Ma'am, may I remind you, this is a library."

Ginny's rich laugh made his dragon scurry around in excitement. "That's not what you said the last time we were here." Sauntering over to him, she took the book from his hand and put it aside. "Care to have a repeat of—oh!"

He pinned her up against the shelves, enjoying the zing of excitement racing up his spine. In the last three days since the bond had formed, they'd made love on his bed, his couch, the shower, and even outside while going on another hike. While each moment with her had been amazing, that first time always replayed in his mind. He wanted to push her up against the shelves again, though maybe this time, he'd tease her first before making her beg for what she wanted.

"Gideon," she moaned as he nibbled on her neck.

"Hmmm?"

"I—oh yes, right there."

"Gods, you're so beautiful and sexy and all mine," he growled as he slipped a hand under her shirt, going straight up to cup her breast.

"Yes."

"Ginny, I need—"

"Gideon!" called a voice from the other side of the shelves. "Are you in here?"

He froze. "One moment, Wesley!" With a disappointed sigh, he removed his hand from her person and ran it through his hair. "I guess that teaches us, huh?"

She grinned at him. "Maybe we can sneak back in here later."

"Not a bad idea." He waggled his eyebrows at her.

"It's a date, babe." She linked her arm through his. "C'mon, let's go say hi to Wesley."

They walked out to the main room, where sure enough, Wesley was already taking his books out from his bag and placing them onto the large table.

"Hey, Wes," Ginny greeted. "How was school?"

"Great," he said.

"I have some news for you," she began. "Though you've probably already guessed it—but, I'm staying in the Northern Isles."

Wesley's head shot up, the rest of his body freezing in place. "Y-you are?"

"Yes." She slipped an arm around Gideon's waist. "I'm in the mates zone, after all." She winked at him.

"I knew it!" Wesley jumped out of his chair and launched himself into her side.

"*Oomph!*" Ginny winced, but placed an arm around him to hold him close.

Wesley looked up at her adoringly. "I'm so glad you're staying, Ginny."

"Me, too, Wes." She ruffled his hair and smiled down at him.

Gideon's dragon let out a miffed snort of jealousy, but he reminded it that Ginny was theirs, now and forever. He placed an arm around her, the warmth in his chest sending his dragon preening with happiness.

Once they had mated, they knew of course, that they had to find a way to be together. Ginny said she'd quit The Agency, but that didn't sound much like a compromise if she was leaving everything behind, so he offered to quit the Dragon Guard once the trainees were ready to move up. Then she objected to *that* plan, and for a while it seemed they would not be able to find a compromise.

In the end, the solution came from Christina Lennox, who understood what it was like to be mated. So, she offered Ginny a new position—as liaison and agent-in-charge of the newly-formed Shifter Protection Agency Northern Isles Bureau. They had worked out the details and finally made it official when King Aleksei signed the Memorandum of Agreement last night, and they all celebrated in the royal apartments. And now, she already had two assignments— help Gideon find the lost prince and the cure for The Wand.

"And I'm glad you're his mate, Ginny," Wesley added.

"You are?" Gideon had asked Ginny a few days ago if maybe Wesley had a crush on her, and she said that Poppy had said that too. The boy wasn't very affectionate, at least not with the adults in his life, but he acted differently toward her. But she said that her own lioness felt protective of him and maybe in turn he felt a kinship toward her because he had never been around female shifters before, much less another feline.

"Of course I am. You're my best friend, Gideon," Wesley proclaimed matter-of-factly. "I just want you to be happy."

A different kind of emotion thickened his throat, making it difficult to speak. He'd always been withdrawn and a loner while growing up. Sure, some people might say Niklas was his best friend. They were close, being twins, but over the years, their interests had diverged, and Gideon found that didn't really have anyone to share his hobbies and pursuits with. So, he supposed that, yes, Wesley was his best friend too.

Ginny squeezed his waist, and from the look she gave him and the gathering moisture in her eyes, he knew she felt every emotion he did through their bond. It was an amazing feeling, something he'd never thought he'd ever experience but now he did, thanked the gods every day for it.

"Well, we should get started," Ginny declared, rubbing at the corner of her eye with her knuckle. "That's why I'm here, after all, to help Gideon with his homework."

Gideon nodded to the laptop and books set up on the other side of the table. "All right, I have all the material about the lost prince with me."

As Wesley started on his schoolwork, Gideon and Ginny sat side by side, peering at his laptop. Today, he would be getting her up to speed about the Grand Duke Aleksandr. After giving her a rundown of the case, he showed her all his research and maps, as well as the transcript from the witness.

She scratched at her chin. "Hmmm."

"What is it?"

"This transcript ... there's something weird ... ah!" She moved the cursor on the screen to highlight one of the words in Ukrainian and then right-clicked it to open another browser. "I thought so."

"What is it?" The browser showed the translation of a word. "Lizard?"

"Yeah." She tapped the word with her finger. "*Jaščarka*. It's Belarusian for lizard. It must have gotten translated into 'reptile' by mistake. It's possible that if your witness lives on the border of Belarus and Ukraine, he code-switches between the two languages."

"Could be. Also, I think the private investigator who found the witness may have translated it to Russian first for Princess Natalia, then she had it translated into English before sending it us, which could further muddle the transcript. But how did you know?"

"I spent some time working at a private zoo outside Minsk," she said nonchalantly.

"A what?" He was still getting used to these strange answers or quips she sometimes gave that reflected her adventurous, nomadic life.

"Long story. Tell you later." She scanned the rest of the interview. "Ah, here's another one. 'Pure' should be 'pearl.'"

"Pearl light?"

"Maybe pearly light? Like that rainbow iridescent sheen pearls have?"

"That doesn't make sense though. What else didn't make it into the translation?"

"One more ... there." Another browser window popped up and showed the word for 'feather.'

"Feathery wings?"

"Huh." Her eyes narrowed. "You know, before coming here, I'd only seen one kind of dragon. I never knew there were different kinds until I saw yours. And you and Sybil look nothing alike. You're more snake-like, while she's like the traditional kind of dragon we know from stories. And your wings are smaller and remind me of a bat's."

"What are you getting at?"

"How many other types of dragons are there? Because it sounds to me, this is a different kind of dragon with a lizard's body, feathery wings, and pearly scales."

"I've never heard of such a dragon, but whatever it is, it doesn't sound like a water dragon at all." That meant that the lead from the princess had been wrong. The dragon the witness spotted hadn't been one of their own. It might not even be a dragon, after all.

"Aw, cheer up, babe." She tipped his chin. "Hey, I could be wrong. Or the witness's sight or memory might be faulty. How about we keep digging? What do we know about this place where this dragon was seen?"

"Hold on." He tapped a few keys on the laptop to bring up a popular online map application, then zoomed in. "According to the GPS data the PI sent us, it should be around here. There." He pointed at a spot on the map.

"Do you have a map of where Zaratena used to be?"

"Sure." He opened one of the images from the folder in his files. "It was hard to find a detailed map of the country, but we actually had it in the archives, so I was able to scan it."

Turning the laptop towards her, she swiftly tapped on the keys. Her golden brows knitted together. "Huh."

"What is it?"

She turned the screen to him. "Look. At the lake in both maps."

The two images were pulled up side by side, showing the large body of water. Though one was in full color and the other in black and white, the two seemed almost identical. Except for one detail.

"Did you see it?" she asked, excited.

"I—why, yes."

In the black and white map was a tiny island in the middle. The internet map, on the other hand, showed no island. He switched from the normal map view to satellite and even topographical, but there was no island to be seen.

"Only the old one shows the island."

"But that's impossible." He scratched at his head. "Princess Natalia's private investigator didn't say anything about an island in the lake. And this map is updated regularly by the most sophisticated satellite system on earth. Why wouldn't it show the island in the middle? Maybe it's a mistake. Some map makers put fake features on their map to prevent plagiarism."

"The Northern Isles doesn't show up on the internet map, either." It was Wesley who spoke up.

"What?" Ginny asked. "It doesn't?"

The boy, who was looking over at them from his books, nodded. "I tried looking for it before Mum and I came here, but it doesn't show up on the satellite maps. I asked Rorik about it. He says it might be because of the veil."

"Veil?" Ginny's lips pursed together. "What veil?"

Gideon forgot that Her Majesty had flown in Ginny, so she wouldn't have felt the veil when they came in. "The Northern Isles is protected by a magical veil that makes it invisible to those outside of it, including satellite cameras. No one knows how it works, but our oral traditions say it's been here even before the first water dragons arrived."

Wesley nodded. "According to my history teacher, the ancestors of the water dragons had lost their home in a Great War. What remained of their tribe flew around the earth forty times before they came upon The Northern Isles. Somehow, they could see through the magical veil and so they settled here."

Her jaw dropped. "That's it! That island in the middle of the lake is there—we just can't see it. No one can. Except for water dragons."

"The magic that exists here could exist there. It's not impossible." His heart drummed in his chest. "We should have checked the lake personally instead of relying on this private investigator. All this time ... *pusen*, you're a genius." Unable to help himself, he kissed her long and hard.

Wesley cleared his throat, making them pull apart. "Are you going to find the lost prince now?"

"I'm not sure, but we're much closer." He glanced at Ginny. "We must speak to the king at once." Finally, real progress on this case. And all thanks to his beautiful, brilliant mate.

"Wow, you look like you're really excited about this," Ginny remarked. "Books and research really get your motor running, huh?"

"I'm afraid this is about as thrilling as my life gets," he said. "Are you all right with the fact that your mate is a boring old scholar and not someone more adventurous you could travel with?"

She let out a snort. "Baby, I've seen the world. I had a great time, but it was different."

"And now?"

The smile on her face lit up his very soul. "And now, I have a brand-new adventure—you."

EPILOGUE

TWO WEEKS LATER ...

The tiny mountain town nestled somewhere between Ukraine and Belarus was so remote that it didn't even have a name on the maps. According to Princess Natalia's private investigator, it took him three days to get there, including six hours driving up a narrow mountain highway. Ginny had never been more thankful to have her very own dragon to fly them there that cut down travel time to a fraction of that.

However, it still took them the better part of the day to find the location the PI had described, and by the time they landed on the large clearing just outside town, the sun was sinking fast in the west.

"Finally." She slipped out of Gideon's dragon's arms when her feet touched the ground. "I thought we'd never find this place. Whew!" Her lioness, on the other hand, had enjoyed the flight and being so close to their mate's dragon. With all the work they had done in the last two weeks to prepare for this trip, they hardly had any leisure time to shift and play together.

Now-human arms wrapped around her again. "Are you

all right, *pusen?*" Gideon asked, concerned. "You must be exhausted."

"She's exhausted?" Niklas exclaimed as he shifted back beside them. "She didn't even do any of the flying."

Ginny wrinkled her nose at him. "Hey, who invited you anyway?"

"Duh, obviously King Aleksei knows you'll need my brilliant mind to crack this case," he retorted. "And gods know you'll never get anything done with you guys making goo-goo eyes at each other all the time."

"Dragon brain!"

"Tuna breath!"

"Now, now, children," Gideon began. "We agreed to get along on this trip."

"She started it."

"You provoked me."

Gideon massaged the bridge of his nose with his thumb and forefinger. "C'mon, let's go check out that town before it gets too late." He placed an arm around Ginny and guided her forward.

Ginny allowed him to lead her, then turned back toward Niklas and stuck her tongue out at him and crossed her eyes. Surprisingly, that made the Dragon Guard laugh aloud, a sound that had been rare in the last two weeks and made hope flare in her. Gideon faltered in his steps, his face going blank for a second. She hip-checked him and raised a brow at him smugly, as if to say *I told you so.*

"All right, you told me so," he grumbled.

The king and queen had been surprised when Niklas insisted on coming along, but Ginny not so much, as she knew he'd been needing a distraction. Apparently, one of his frequent on-again-off-again girlfriends had somehow sunken her claws into Niklas recently. Ginny had never met this woman, but Gideon obviously disliked her and predicated that, like the many other times they'd gotten back together, this wasn't going to end well.

And it didn't.

Niklas had been so morose and mopey the past couple of days, she hardly recognized him. Gideon tried to help his twin get out of his funk, but did so by walking on eggshells around him, treating him like some fragile doll. Ginny, however, had taken the opposite approach, doing her best to needle and provoke Niklas. Gideon had doubted her methods, but she had a feeling it was the only way to get through to him, and while at first, he didn't respond, but slowly he rose to the bait. And now she felt a breakthrough with the return of his laughter, and the mood around him lightened considerably.

Comfortable silence settled over them as they trudged up the dirt road that led into the main town. Well, calling it a town was rather generous—it was more like a village, with a single paved street where about a dozen cottages and small buildings lined one side. As they stood at the bottom of the hill, they all looked at each other.

"What's the next step?" Niklas asked.

"This is the closest town to the lake, but it's a hike to get there," Gideon began. "I'm eager to go fly over there now, but we don't know what to expect from the missing Dragon Guard—or whoever or whatever creature is living there."

After much research, they still hadn't found any such dragon with pearly scales and feathered wings, nor any kind of fabled creature matching that description, so they planned to take as many precautions as they could.

"They might be hostile," Ginny added. "I say we stay the night here and check out the lake in the morning. Go on foot just to be sure. We have to take the careful and stealthy approach."

"All right, let's go find somewhere to sleep for the night," Niklas said.

"I'll go around town and see what I can find," Ginny began. "I've brushed up on my Belarusian, so hopefully, I can manage."

"Be careful, *pusen.*" Gideon squeezed her hand.

"You know I will." And that was one of the reasons she loved Gideon so much. While he cared for her, he didn't suffocate her or insist that he do things for her. Instead, he trusted in her abilities.

"That looks like some kind of bar or restaurant." Niklas nodded to the two-story building in the middle of the row with green painted shutters and a faded sign hanging outside the door. "Let's go get some food."

They parted ways, and Ginny began to knock on the doors along the street. It took her a while as the first couple of people basically shut their doors on her or chased her away by screaming what she could roughly translate as obscenities. Eventually, she found an old woman whose eyes gleamed when Ginny flashed the cash in her pocket. *Should have started with that,* she thought wryly.

After securing two rooms in the woman's house, she made her way to the bar, walking slower than usual, fatigue making her limbs loose and heavy. *I could use a real meal and a sit down.* By the time she was pushing the creaky wooden door to get in, she was already dreaming of a hot bowl of borscht.

However, the moment she stepped in, her lioness immediately went on alert. Tension hung in the air like a thick, heavy blanket, and her gaze scanned the room for her mate. Sure enough, she found him, standing right behind Niklas by the bar, facing off against a group of men.

Oh, brother.

Swiftly but carefully, she strode up beside Gideon. She was about to ask him what was going on when she noticed the pretty, dark-haired woman in between Niklas and the group of men. Oh, brother indeed.

"The lady said she didn't want to be disturbed," Niklas said through gritted teeth. "You should leave her alone."

"I said I'm fine!" the woman retorted. "Don't need your help." She glared at the group of men and then Niklas. "Any of you."

Ginny blinked, realizing the young woman spoke English. "Miss," she began. "Is everything all right?"

"Yeshhhh," she slurred. As she let go of the bar, she teetered forward, and Ginny quickly grabbed her by the forearms before she fell over.

"Whoa there." The smell of alcohol from her breath made her wince and her inner lioness snort in disapproval. "Maybe we should get you home?"

She lifted her head and grimaced. "Too far. Never get there on foot."

"We'll give you a ride home," Niklas offered.

"Nooooo!" the woman whined. "No fun there!"

Ginny sighed. Niklas could never resist a woman in need. That knight in shining armor attitude that would never have flown with her, if they had been mates. "All right." She turned to the other men and spoke a few polite words telling them they were leaving to escort the young lady home. Thankfully, they had somehow understood her broken Belarusian and dispersed.

"Let's get out of here." *Guess that borscht would have to wait.*

Slinging an arm under the young woman, Ginny led her away from the bar, which would have been a hell of a whole lot easier if she was cooperative. Instead, she kicked and screamed and dug her heels in.

"Don't ... wanna go ... home!" she screamed.

Ginny blew out a breath. "I really didn't want to do this, but you've forced my hand." Bending down, she lifted the woman over her shoulder.

"Everything'sh upshide down!" she squealed. "Let go, mean lady!"

As she struggled, Ginny kept her grip tight until they got out and far away from the restaurant. Her screeches made Ginny's ears ring, so she put her down—flat on her ass on the ground. "God, even Prince Alric is better behaved than you and he's two," she said, recalling her conversation with Sybil about drunk adults being like children.

The young woman howled as she attempted to get up to her feet, swaying unsteadily, her hands grasping at the air in an attempt to stay steady. "You've met a prince? I ... I am a p-p-rin ..." She blinked and twisted her lips, opening and closing them like a fish. "Prinsh ... princh ... pranch? Uh, whaddaya call a girl prince?"

"Princess?"

She giggled. "Princess!" Then her body pitched forward,

and once again, Ginny caught her on time. This time, she passed out completely.

"Princess, right." Ginny rolled her eyes. "How drunk was she?"

"Very," Niklas sighed. "Already three sheets to the wind by the time we walked in. But she didn't get loud until after those guys started harassing her."

"And you had to get involved, of course," Gideon said drolly.

"What, I was supposed to let those guys take advantage of her?"

"You don't even know her."

"Guys, what are we going to do about her?" Ginny asked. The two gave her identical blank looks. "Ugh. All right. Give me a hand."

The twins held her up while Ginny searched her pants pockets and under her sweater just in case. *No wallet or ID.* "Damn it."

"What do we do now?" Niklas asked. "Should go around to each house and check if they know her."

"Something tells me if she were local, the men in there wouldn't have bothered her or one of the restaurant workers would have called her relatives by now," Gideon said.

"True." Ginny thought for a moment. "Well, we can't leave her out on the streets." She shook her head and blew out an exasperated breath. "I guess she's bunking with us for the night."

Thankfully, the old woman who rented them the rooms didn't say anything when they came back with the passed out young woman. Her mate had grumbled the entire time as they ate their dinner, which consisted of the protein bars they had packed for the trip. But she'd assured him that it was only one night, and tomorrow, when the young woman sobered up, they could send her on her way, and then head out to investigate the mysterious island on the lake. Ginny shared one bed with her while Gideon and Niklas bunked in together in the other room. Her lioness had protested, because ever since they had mated, she had slept soundly each night in his arms, as if his mere presence chased her bad dreams away. Good thing however, was that she was so tired that she immediately fell asleep.

As she woke, Ginny stretched and yawned, trying to brush the cobwebs of sleep from her brain. "Good morning, babe," she greeted as she usually did every morning. Then she remembered Gideon wasn't next to her. Ah, right. She shared her bed with Princess Can't-Hold-Her-Liquor.

Ginny reached out next to her, but her hand only landed on an empty pillow. She shot up and looked around the small room. There was no sign of her. "Christ Almighty!"

Tossing the thin sheet aside, she scrambled out of bed. Dashing out, she headed straight for the door across, not bothering to knock as she pushed it open. "Gideon! Niklas! Is she here?"

In a flash, Gideon was at her side, hair sticking up and wearing only pajama bottoms. "What's wrong?" She could feel his dragon go on full alert, ready to fight. Her lioness purred in delight, as it had missed sleeping next to their mate.

Niklas, who'd slept on the floor, lifted his head from the pillow sleepily. "What's going on?"

"Your little girlfriend is gone!" Ginny said, exasperated.

"Who?"

"You know, Her Royal Highness, Princess Hammered Off Her Ass."

He blinked. "Crap, where did she go?"

"Maybe she went home?" Gideon offered.

Niklas pushed himself off the floor. "I guess that's possible."

Ginny thought for a moment. "Well, if you guys aren't worried, I won't be either." It was already light outside, and she supposed the young woman was sobered up by now and found her way home. "How about we go get some breakfast and then head out to the lake?"

After getting ready for the day, Ginny went downstairs to talk to the old woman. Another couple of euros got them some bread, cheese, and tea, and once their bellies were full, prepared for their hike.

Following a paper map Gideon had printed out, they headed toward where the lake should be. From the end of the single road in town, they had to take a dirt road that turned east, and then follow a path deep in the forest which should lead them to the shores of the lake.

"Are we there yet?" Niklas asked.

"No, and you asked five minutes ago," Ginny said, rolling her eyes. "C'mon, it looks like we should go this way."

"Isn't it strange that there's no road to this lake?" Gideon asked. "It's the nearest water source to the town, plus, there's probably plenty of fish in that lake."

"Yeah, maybe in the olden days they had some kind of

dirt road," Ginny began. "But with modernization, the town has running water and electricity, plus with the population being so small, the government might not think building a road was practical or necessary."

"True," Gideon said. "Oh, look! I think we're almost there."

Sure enough, when Ginny looked ahead, she saw the end of the forest and dots of blue sky. "Thank God!"

They hurried out of the dirt path, and soon they stood by the edge of a lake, the water so clear that a mirror image of the mountains behind them reflected off the surface.

"By Odin, it's exquisite!" Gideon proclaimed.

"Yeah." Niklas stepped forward and took a deep breath. "I swear I've never felt anything so ... so ... what the fuck?"

"It is—huh?" Ginny stopped short. "Niklas?"

"Over there." Niklas's amber eyes darkened and narrowed.

She followed his gaze, just to their right, where there was a small rocky outcropping over the lake. A figure stood right at the edge, arms spread. "Is that—"

"It's her," Gideon said.

"What the hell is she doing?" Niklas grit his teeth.

Ginny used her shifter vision to focus and recognized her immediately. Sure enough, it was the young woman from last night.

She was wearing the same sweater and pants and kept her arms spread out. "I'm sorry!" she screamed. "Please, I'm so sorry I ran away, I just want to go home."

"What is she screaming about?" Niklas asked.

"Shh!" Ginny held her hand up. "Wait a—no!"

The woman suddenly leapt from the rocks. Ginny's

stomach jumped into her chest and Niklas screamed in horror.

"No!" He immediately took off and jumped into the lake, the reflections of the mountains rippling and disappearing as he disturbed the calm waters.

"Niklas!" But before she could dash after him, a bright flash of light blinded her. "What the—" She sucked in a breath as her vision cleared. "Holy Moly!"

From out of nowhere, a large, winged creature material- ized and swooped down, catching the young woman just before she hit the water. She let out a whoop, clung onto the creature's back, and they flew off before disappearing into thin air.

Slowly, she turned toward Gideon. "Did you—"

"I did—"

"Was it—"

"A lizard—no—dragon with pearly scales and feathered wings," he finished, his jaw dropping. "We need to—Gods- dammit, Niklas!"

A loud splash made her whip her head around. Sure enough, Niklas's dragon shot out from beneath the surface of the lake, and then flew off toward the center.

"Where the hell does he think he's going?"

Gideon slapped his hand on his forehead. "Where else? To rescue the princess."

Damn Niklas and his propensity to be the knight in shining armor. "All right." She straightened her shoulders. "Looks like we're not taking the careful and stealthy approach after all."

"I'm going to skin him alive," Gideon ground out.

"And you said that being mated to you would be boring because I'd never go off on another adventure."

"When this is all over, I'll take you on a proper, long honeymoon," he blurted out.

The word honeymoon made her heart skip a beat. "Honeymoon, huh?" She smirked at him. "I didn't hear you ask me a certain question first."

He grinned back sheepishly. "I was waiting for the right time. Preferably not while my twin is about to cause serious menace."

"Ask me again later, then." She stepped into his arms, feeling the presence of his dragon. Once again, her lioness mewled in happiness, knowing they were going flying with their mate. "Maybe it'll work out and Niklas won't get us into any trouble."

"Somehow, I highly doubt that."

And because she knew her future brother-in-law too well, she did too. "All right, babe, time to hit the skies."

Dear Reader,

Thanks for starting this adventure with me!

I hope you enjoyed Ginny and Gideon's story. If you want to read a hot, sexy bonus scene that happens right after the end:

http://aliciamontgomeryauthor.com/mailing-list/

You'll get access to ALL the bonus materials from all my books and my **FREE** novella **The Last Blackstone Dragon.**

Plus, turn the page for a preview of Dragon Guard Knight, the next book in the Dragon Guard Series.

Thanks again for reading!

All my love,

Alicia

Niklas had done some pretty outrageous things in the past to distract himself from heartbreak, but going to a mountain town in the middle of nowhere in Eastern Europe certainly took the cake.

His inner dragon snorted ruefully as if saying, *I told you so.*

Yeah, yeah. He'd heard his dragon's protests a hundred times before. But really, he thought that *this time*, getting back together with Karina was a good idea. This time, they actually lasted a whole three days before things went downhill.

"After you," his twin brother, Gideon, said as he gestured to the dilapidated door. The sign above it was so faded that even if Niklas spoke the local language, he wouldn't have been able to read it.

"Why me?" he asked.

"It was your idea."

Niklas shrugged and pushed the door open, the rusty old hinges squeaking in protest. He was hungry and tired from flying the whole day, and a hot meal sounded good right about now. They were lucky there was even any kind of eating establishment in this one-horse town. *If they even had a single horse around here.* And calling it a town was generous. It was more like a village, with one main road and a few houses and buildings. But this is where they were supposed to go, and Niklas had only come along because it beat moping around back home in the Northern Isles.

The place was nearly empty, save for a few patrons by the bar—a lone figure at one end wearing a cap and sweater and a group of men on the other, but they seemed too engrossed in their loud conversation to notice the two new people who had come in. Niklas and Gideon hunkered down in a table in the farthest corner.

"I don't think this place has a menu." Niklas glanced around. "Should we wait for Ginny to make an order?" Their third companion and Gideon's mate, Ginny Russel, had gone off in search of lodgings for the evening.

Gideon fished his phone out of his pocket. "I can use my translator app and see if I can at least get some drinks. But first, let me send a message to Rorik that we've made it."

Niklas drummed his fingers on the table. "Do you think this is the place? I mean, this lake nearby?"

"According to the map, it is," Gideon replied, not looking up from his phone. "Damn ... signal's pretty weak. Can't even get high-speed data."

"But do you think we'll find the lost prince there?"

His twin pursed his lips and put the phone on the table. "All the clues have led us here. So, we'll find out soon enough."

Though Gideon and Niklas were Dragon Guards for

King Aleksei of the Northern Isles, they were on a special mission to find the king's long-lost uncle. Prince Sasha of Zaratena supposedly perished in a revolution about sixty years ago, along with an unnamed Dragon Guard who had been sent to protect him. But the last remaining member of his family, his aunt, Princess Natalia, hadn't given up hope that he might still be alive. And after all this time, her optimism had finally paid off as her search uncovered clues that the lost prince might be in this small mountain town between Belarus and Ukraine. A witness had seen a dragon flying over the lake, and when Gideon and Ginny did further research, they found old maps that showed a mysterious island in the middle of the lake that could not be seen on any satellite.

Niklas chewed at his lip. "What do you think is on that island? And do you think the creature that witness saw is the missing Dragon Guard?"

"I'm not sure, quite frankly." Gideon frowned. "Surely it's no coincidence that the same magical veil that protects this island is the same kind of magic that protects the Northern Isles. Only a water dragon would be able to see it."

After putting the clues together, they put together a working theory that the Dragon Guard assigned to Prince Sasha had somehow escaped the revolutionists and flew him off to safety on this island. Of course, if he was alive, no one knew why Prince Sasha hadn't come forward, plus there was the issue that no one in the Northern Isles could even remember who this mysterious Dragon Guard was.

"Well, we'll get our answers tomorrow," Niklas said. They had agreed to investigate the island in the morning and take a stealthier approach. After all, they had no idea what to expect. If there was a dragon or some kind of creature guarding the island, there was a chance it might not be friendly.

"Or this could all be a wild goose chase," Gideon replied glumly.

"Relax, bro. Don't worry, it'll all work out." He sent his twin an encouraging smile. "Besides, if we don't find the prince here, then we'll go back to the drawing board, and you'll find him eventually." And Niklas had no doubt about that because Gideon was one of the smartest men he knew.

"I don't—"

A sharp, feminine cry made them both freeze. Turning his head toward the bar, Niklas gritted his teeth as he saw the female surrounded by three large men. He didn't notice that the lone figure hunched over a drink had been female as she had her back to them. But it was obvious now as her cap was gone, and a long braid of dark hair swung down her shoulders. He shot to his feet.

"Niklas," Gideon warned. "Don't even—"

But Niklas didn't hear the end of that sentence as he used his shifter speed to stand in front of the girl. "What's going on here?"

The largest of the men—a hulking creature with shoulders as large as boulders—said something in the local language that Niklas didn't understand, but he could get the gist of it from the harsh tone.

"I'm fine. Thoshe bashtards just need to stop dish-turbing me." She glared at the men.

Niklas blinked and whirled around. "You speak English?"

"And French, German, Russian, Belarusian, and ... and ..." Her eyes glazed over. "What was I saying?"

The stench of alcohol from her breath was evident. "You're drunk."

"Sh-sho what?" she slurred. "And who the hell are you anyway?"

"I'm just trying to help you—"

A hand snaked around Niklas and attempted to grab the girl. Rage burst through him, and he pulled the man's arm away. "The lady said she didn't want to be disturbed." There was nothing Niklas hated more than a man who disrespected women. "You should leave her alone."

"I said I'm fine!" the woman retorted. "Don't need your help." She glared at the group of men and then Niklas. "Any of you."

"Miss," came a voice from behind. It was Ginny. "Is everything all right?" Though her demeanor was calm, Niklas could feel the lioness within her, ready in case things went down.

"Yeshhhh," the woman slurred. As she let go of the bar, she teetered forward.

"Whoa there." Ginny quickly caught her and winced. "Maybe we should get you home?"

She lifted her head and grimaced. "Too far. Never get there on foot."

"We'll give you a ride home," Niklas offered.

"Nooooo!" the woman whined. "No fun there!"

"All right." Ginny turned to the men and said a few words in what Niklas guessed was Belarusian. Apparently, it was one of the languages his brother's mate spoke as before she came to the Northern Isles, she had been some-what of a wanderer. Whatever she said, it seemed to appease the men and they dispersed. She turned back to them. "Let's get out of here." She slung an arm under the young woman and began to lead her away, but unfortunately, she attempted to wiggle from Ginny's grasp and dug her heels into the floor when the lioness shifter attempted to drag her away.

"Don't ... wanna go ... home!" she screamed.

Ginny blew out a breath. "I really didn't want to do this, but you've forced my hand." Bending down, she lifted the woman over her shoulder.

"Everything'sh upshide down!" she squealed. "Let go, mean lady!"

"I didn't know she had it in her," Niklas whispered to his twin, who only attempted to suppress a grin as they followed Ginny and the unruly girl outside of the bar.

Seemingly annoyed of the girl's incessant screeching, Ginny dumped the young woman on the ground. "God, even Prince Alric is better behaved than you, and he's two!"

The young woman howled as she attempted to get up to her feet, swaying unsteadily, her hands grasping at the air in an attempt to stay steady. "You've met a prince? I ... I am a p-p-rin ..." She blinked and twisted her lips, opening and closing them like a fish's. "Prinsh ... princh ... pranch? Uh, whaddaya call a girl prince?"

"Princess?"

She giggled. "Princess!" Then her body pitched forward, and once again, Ginny caught her. This time, she passed out completely.

"Princess, right." Ginny rolled her eyes. "How drunk was she?"

"Very. Already three sheets to the wind by the time we walked in," Niklas recalled the empty bottle on the bar in front of the girl. "But she didn't get loud until after those guys started harassing her."

"And you had to get involved, of course," Gideon said drolly.

Niklas put his hands up. "What, I was supposed to let those guys take advantage of her?"

"You don't even know her," his twin retorted.

"Guys, what are we going to do about her?" Ginny asked. When neither man answered, she let out an exasperated grunt. "Ugh. All right. Give me a hand."

Niklas grabbed the woman's left arm, and Gideon did the same with the right. As they propped her up, Ginny searched through the woman's person and found nothing. "Damn it."

"What do we do now?" Niklas asked. "Should go around to each house and check if they know her."

"Something tells me if she were local, the men in there wouldn't have bothered her, or one of the restaurant workers would have called her relatives by now," Gideon said.

"True." Ginny thought for a moment. "Well, we can't leave her out on the streets." She shook her head and blew out an exasperated breath. "I guess she's bunking with us for the night."

Niklas carried the young woman down the hill, toward the house where Ginny had secured them lodgings for the evening. "There're two rooms upstairs," she said as she knocked on the door. "Take her to the one with the big bed, I'll stay there with her for the night, then once Princess Three Sheets to the Wind sobers up, she can be on her way."

They entered the home, and Ginny greeted the old woman, who nodded at them curiously but said nothing. Heading up the stairs, they located the rooms and Niklas placed the woman on the bed. He took off her muddy boots, then hoisted her legs onto the mattress. "Ginny can take care of the rest of her."

"She doesn't look older than twenty," Gideon remarked.

"Probably because she's not wearing an inch of makeup." The girl's skin looked pristine, though. Niklas couldn't recall what color her eyes were.

"Well, you're the expert on women," Gideon teased.

"Ha ha." He waved his hand at his twin. "No sir. No more women for me." Not for a while, at least.

Gideon's expression fell. "I'm sorry about Karina."

He flinched at the name. "It's fine."

"No, it's not. Also, I know I've been neglecting you," he said sheepishly. "These past couple of weeks. Because of Ginny."

"What?" Niklas couldn't believe Gideon would think that way. "Bro, no! I'm happy you found your mate. Really, I am." Not every shifter found their destined mate, but his brother was one of the lucky ones who did. And Niklas really was glad that Gideon and Ginny found each other. He just wished he had someone like that too.

"C'mon," Gideon gestured to the door. "Let's see if we can find something to eat. That bartender didn't seem too happy with us, and I have no intention of slinking back there to beg for a meal."

Niklas let out a long breath. Still, he would rather be here in this dank little farmhouse eating protein bars for dinner than risk having to run into his ex back home. His inner dragon huffed, agreeing with him. His dragon had always been indifferent to his girlfriends in the past and just women in general, but it hated Karina in particular. Or perhaps it, too, felt envy that their twin had found the other half of their soul while they were still woefully alone.

Pushing those thoughts aside, he followed Gideon out of the room. "I think we have some protein bars in the bag. We can have those for dinner."

———

Niklas was so deep into his dream about surfing back in California that the sound of the door slamming against the wall and his brother's thundering voice barely woke him up. "What's wrong?" he asked, yawning as he lifted his head from the pillow. He slept on a blanket on the floor as the twin bed barely had room for Gideon. Seeing it was his fault his brother wasn't snuggling with his mate for the night, Niklas graciously gave up the soft mattress.

"Your little girlfriend is gone!" Ginny said, exasperated.

His girlfriend? "Who?"

"You know, Her Royal Highness, Princess Hammered Off Her Ass."

Oh. *Her.* He blinked. "Crap, where did she go?"

"Maybe she went home?" Gideon offered.

Niklas pushed himself off the floor. "I guess that's possible."

Ginny's lips pursed. "Well, if you guys aren't worried, I won't be either. How about we go find some breakfast and then head out to the lake?"

As Ginny headed downstairs, Niklas and Gideon got ready for the day. Thankfully, Ginny was able to convince their hostess to serve them some bread, cheese, and tea, and soon they were on their way.

"Are we there yet?" Niklas asked.

They had followed the single road out of town, then onto a dirt road that turned east, leading into a thick patch of forest. According to Gideon's map, if they continued this way, they should hit the shore of the lake.

"No, and you asked five minutes ago," Ginny said, rolling her eyes. "C'mon, it looks like we should go this way."

"Isn't it strange that there's no road to this lake?" Gideon asked. "It's the nearest water source to the town, plus there's probably plenty of fish in that lake."

"Yeah, maybe in the olden days, they had some kind of dirt road," Ginny began. "But with modernization, the town has running water and electricity, plus with the population being so small, the government might not think building a road was practical or necessary."

"True," Gideon said. "Oh look! I think we're almost there."

Sure enough, up ahead was the end of the forest and dots of blue sky. "Thank God!" Ginny exclaimed.

They hurried out of the dirt path, and soon they stood by the edge of a lake, the water so clear that a mirror image of the mountains behind them reflected off the surface.

"By Odin, it's exquisite!" Gideon proclaimed.

"Yeah." Niklas stepped forward and took a deep breath. "I swear I've never felt anything so ... so ..." Something in the distance caught his eye on a small rocky outcropping over the lake. "What the fuck?"

"It is—huh?" Ginny's head snapped toward him. "Niklas?"

Was that ... *oh shit, it was!* A figure stood at the edge of the outcropping, arms spread, shouting up at the sky. "Over there."

Ginny followed his gaze. "Is that—"

"It's her," Gideon said.

Yup, that was definitely the girl from last night. Same hair, same sweater and pants. "What the hell is she doing?" Niklas grit his teeth.

"I'm sorry!" the girl screamed. "Please, I'm so sorry I ran away, I just want to go home."

"What is she screaming about?" Niklas asked.

"Shhh!" Ginny held her hand up. "Wait a—no!"

The woman suddenly leapt from the rocks, and Niklas screamed in horror.

"No!" He dashed forward, pushing his dragon out as fast as he could. Diving into the lake, he barely felt the cold water as his inner animal burst from his skin. The dragon swam toward the bottom of the outcropping, waiting for the woman's body to break through the water, but seconds passed, and there was only peaceful silence.

What the fuck?

The dragon looked up, then broke through the surface. A white flash blinded them for a moment, but the water dragon didn't flinch or attempt to shield their eyes. No, it leapt out of the water, toward the flash.

What the hell is that?

It was some kind of winged creature, slightly smaller than Niklas's dragon, but its body was covered with pearly scales. And its wings! Much larger than his, and they were white with feathers at the edges. For some reason, his heart rioted in his chest. But in a split second, it disappeared into thin air.

His dragon bolted in the direction where the white creature had gone. *It's gone!* he told his dragon. *Let's go back—*

But his inner animal didn't listen as it shot right after the creature. The white dragon had likely Cloaked itself, a camouflage ability most of their kind shared. But Niklas could still sense its presence, and so did his own dragon, who flew right toward the center of the lake.

We have to go back! The plan was to stakeout the lake first and see if they could locate the island or the barrier. But his dragon continued to fly forward, as if it had a mind of its own. What the hell was happening?

A sudden jolt shook Niklas to the core. He recognized the sensation. *The veil.* It was definitely the same one around the Northern Isles. That confirmed one theory, but where—

Mother Frigga!

As they broke through the veil, something appeared up ahead.

An island in the middle of the lake.

Where the hell were they?

ABOUT THE AUTHOR

Alicia Montgomery has always dreamed of becoming a romance novel writer. She started writing down her stories in now long-forgotten diaries and notebooks, never thinking that her dream would come true. After taking the well-worn path to a stable career, she is now plunging into the world of self-publishing.

 facebook.com/aliciamontgomeryauthor

twitter.com/amontromance

bookbub.com/authors/alicia-montgomery